Murder at the Lighthouse

by

Frances Evesham

An Exham on Sea Mystery

CHAPTER ONE
Under the Lighthouse

The autumn high tide discarded Susie Bennett under the lighthouse, on the beach she'd avoided for twenty years.

Miles of sand stretched on either side, bleak and deserted except for Susie, dog-walker Libby Forest, and a springer spaniel called Shipley. Libby shivered. She should have brought a thicker coat. She tugged the hood further down, against the wind that snapped strands of wet brown hair across her face.

"What's that?" She freed the dog from his lead and squinted ahead. Shipley barked, whiskers quivering, head pointing across the sand, towards the nine stumpy legs of the lighthouse. "Probably just an old sack washed up on the tide. Still, we'd better take a closer look." Sand clumped on Libby's boots. Closer to the lighthouse, where the mud sucked and tugged at the unwary, she picked her way with care, testing every step.

This was no old sack. Shipley nudged Libby's legs and licked her hand, his tongue warm and

1

soft. She rubbed the dog's ears. "It's just a drunk, I think." The drunk's jacket offered less protection against the weather than Libby's anorak. "We'd better wake him." She braced herself for a mouthful of abuse as the sleeping drunk woke, and shook one of the leather-clad arms.

The figure slid noiselessly to the sand. The spaniel nosed it, whining. "Quiet, Shipley." Libby squatted beside the body and brushed sopping wet hair from the icy cheek. "It's a woman." She searched the neck for a pulse. The hollow sensation in Libby's stomach told her what she would find. Shipley howled. Libby staggered up, legs trembling. "What's more, she's dead."

They were still alone on the beach, the only walkers to brave the morning's weather. Libby shivered. "We'd better tell the police." She tugged a mobile phone from an inside pocket and fumbled, jabbing at the numbers.

"Hello, do you need fire, police or ambulance?"

This was only the second corpse Libby had seen. The first, belonging to Trevor, had been laid out at the hospital, triggering a mix of horror and guilty relief.

There was nothing she could do for this woman. Who could it be? A local? No one Libby recognised, but then, she hardly knew anyone: just Marina, Shipley's owner; Frank, the proprietor of the bakery where she worked; and a dozen members of the local history society.

Slim and tiny, the dead woman wore skin-tight jeans. A brown ankle boot encased one foot, but the other was bare, the expensive footwear long gone. The woman's lips were fuller than nature intended. Cosmetic work in the recent past? Drenched hair half-concealed a small, neat face with a turned-up nose. A line of darker hair, along a parting on the side of the head, suggested highlights; a proper salon job, not a do-it-yourself.

Libby peered into the pools of water left stranded under the lighthouse, looking for a handbag, hoping for clues, but the sea had taken that as well.

I shouldn't touch the body again. Libby knew the rules: everyone did. *Don't disturb the scene.* She ought to wait for the police to arrive, but something about the woman's arm, tucked at such an awkward angle into a jacket pocket, nagged at Libby. It wouldn't do any harm just to give it another small nudge, surely?

She twitched the sleeve. The arm jerked. Libby gulped, then took a slow breath. It was just rigor mortis. She pulled again, harder. The stiff hand popped out of the pocket, rigid, fingers pointing to the bleak, wide Somerset sky, and a chunk of plastic tumbled from the jacket. Libby whispered,

3

"Sorry," as though the dead woman could still hear.

The sudden, shocking wail of police sirens brought an officer, younger than her own son, running down the beach. Libby held out one hand, as if to protect the body. "Be careful."

The young, plainclothes officer raised an eyebrow above intense blue eyes and waved an ID card under Libby's nose. "Detective Sergeant Ramshore. Step over there and leave it to us, now, please, madam."

A policewoman in uniform escorted Libby from the beach, leaving the blonde, dead stranger forlorn, a small, plastic ring with a pink stone tumbled beside her on the sand.

CHAPTER TWO

Coffee and Cake

"There's no reason to cancel the meeting." Marina folded her arms, enclosed in the purple sleeves of a wafty silk caftan, across an ample chest. "The police said they'd keep you informed. They'll let you know what they find out."

"Yes, but..." Libby wasn't confident the young officer would bother.

"No, listen to me." Marina was not the newly retired deputy head of the local primary school for nothing. She understood command. "You need a distraction, Libby, or else you'll worry. I know you."

Libby bit back a reply. Marina, leading light of the WI, the music society, the food fair and the local history society, assumed the town's new arrival couldn't make the smallest decision for herself. She'd taken the unsuspecting Libby under her wing and somehow talked her into providing cake for the history society meetings. "Everyone's sure to love it, dear, and they'll all buy your book."

"Hmm. If I ever finish it." Marina waved away

such nonsense. Writing a book about celebration cakes, full of photographs, must be the easiest way possible to make a living. "Anyway, you can practice on us." Libby duly supplied a different, elaborate confection for each meeting. She had to stand on her own feet, now her husband was dead, and she needed all the publicity she could get.

Marina sampled a slice of today's contribution, a pineapple and coconut upside-down cake with a cream cheese frosting. "Mmm. Delicious. Best yet." The doorbell rang. "There you are." She beamed. "It's too late to cancel, now. Angela's here."

Soon, Marina's grand drawing room was full. "Quite a turn-out," Angela Miles murmured in Libby's ear. "Almost everyone's braved the rain, today. News travels fast. Good heavens, even Samantha's gracing us with her presence."

Samantha Watson folded a pair of long legs, sheer black tights hissing as she smoothed a tight pencil skirt over shapely knees. She enjoyed a carefully-constructed reputation as the town's intellectual: a solicitor, she regularly completed the Telegraph crossword. She allowed very few social occasions to take up her valuable time, but today, she'd made an exception. "One of my clients has cancelled her appointment, so I've just popped in for a minute." Samantha smiled, doing the society a favour. "Such a shame, another tragedy on the beach. More visitors stuck in the mud, I suppose."

Allowing Marina to place a slice of cake on her plate, she cut it neatly into tiny squares and popped them, one after another, into a lipsticked mouth, her little pink tongue flicking out to chase stray crumbs. "Quite nice," she pronounced. She allowed her gaze to fall on Libby. "I hear you found the body?"

Libby had no chance to answer, for Marina's excitement overflowed. "Such a shock, finding a body. Honestly, it gave me palpitations, just hearing about it. You must just be in *pieces*, Libby dear." Her voice sunk to a dramatic whisper. "Imagine, a dead body, lying there all night, out on the beach, in such dreadful weather."

Samantha cleared her throat, to focus attention back on herself. "I spoke to Chief Inspector Arnold."

Libby frowned, puzzled. Angela murmured, "That's why she's come, of course. To tell us she's in the know." Angela winked. "Samantha hears all Arnold's secrets." She whispered. "Pillow talk." Libby swallowed a splutter of laughter. She knew Samantha married her handsome, rather dim husband, Ned the local builder, when they were still in their teens.

Angela went on, "Ned came from the old

7

family that used to own the Hall. He's named after on if his ancestors, Sir Benedict, but the title died out years ago and the family sold up. You don't often see Ned and Samantha together, these days."

Samantha, smiled from one expectant face to another. "Stephen, I mean, Chief Inspector Arnold, of course, told me the woman is Susie Bennett."

Marina's jaw dropped. "No. Not Susie?"

Samantha beamed, smug mouth curved in a complacent smile. "That's right, Susie Bennett, the folk singer—or rock singer, was it?" She shrugged elegant, cashmere-clad shoulders. "The Susie Bennett who used to go to school with some of us." She let her eyes rest on Libby, who was never at school with "us." "The Chief Inspector says she committed suicide."

Seriously? He's already decided? Libby pressed her lips together and kept her thoughts to herself.

Everyone in the room seemed to have known the dead woman. Marina gasped. "Oh good gracious me. Susie Bennett! She hasn't been back for years. Whatever was she doing here?"

Angela set down her cup of tea. "Libby, dear, Susie is Exham on Sea's most famous export. She went to the United States and sold millions of records, back in the 80s. She was in a band called Angel's Kiss. I remember, because my name's

Angela. Actually, Angel's Kiss was a cocktail, I believe."

Marina interrupted. "I remember one of their albums. It came with a drinking straw attached to the cover, I think. That lovely song, 'What's In a Name,' was one of the tracks. Susie played the guitar and sang, and there was Guy with a violin and another boy—what was his name, now? Oh yes, James. He was on keyboards."

Samantha fiddled with her pearl necklace. "I don't want to be unkind, but Susie, or Suzanne, as she was in those days, was rather—how can I put it—strange. You know, she had a big voice, big blue eyes, and a great deal of blonde hair, but there was no brain there at all. I mean, she left school with absolutely no qualifications."

"We were all madly jealous of her, to be honest," Angela admitted. "Off we went to University, or started work as trainees at Barclays Bank or Marks and Spencer, while she went to America and made records. She married a fabulously wealthy record producer, but the marriage didn't last long. I don't know about the rest of you, but I haven't seen or heard of her for years." She sighed. "We were rather unkind to her, I'm afraid."

When the teapot was drained and the cake plate empty, the meeting broke up. "Next time," Marina

9

said, "we really must talk about history."

Finally, only George Edwards, the sole male member of the society, remained. He wrapped the last slice of cake in a paper napkin and, breaking his silence, begged Libby to write down the recipe for his wife, at home nursing a cold and laryngitis. "She'll be sorry she missed everything."

CHAPTER THREE

Robert's Discovery

Recessed spotlights picked out the details of Libby's beautifully equipped kitchen as she made coffee, using the state-of-the-art, instant hot water dispenser, installed last week. She pulled out mixing bowls, sieves and scales, and settled to a trial run of the perfect, elaborate, light-as-air cake she was developing. If it turned out as beautifully as she expected, it would make a wonderful cover picture for the book, "Baking at the Beach."

It was this room that persuaded Libby to buy the cottage. Facing south, always either sunny or cosy, perfect for a baking fanatic. Without a qualm, she'd sold Trevor's treasured collection of trains, lavishing every last penny they fetched on her workplace. From the KitchenAid mixer on the granite counter, to the gleaming rows of heavy bottomed pans that hung on the wall near the double-size range cooker, Libby adored every inch of the room.

She'd once confided the dream of opening a patisserie to her husband. Trevor took off his

11

glasses and glared, his nose less than an inch away. "Don't be so stupid." Libby flinched as saliva hit her face. "Throwing good money after bad. Besides, I expect to find you at home when I come back after a hard day." He sneered, replaced the spectacles right on the end of his nose, poured a tumbler of whisky and settled down to read the newspaper's business section. Libby's new kitchen would have been enough to make him choke on his drink.

Tomorrow, she'd start the search for a builder, and get rid of the horrid, 1970s bathroom: the one room in the cottage she hated. The orange tiles made her feel sick every time she saw them.

The phone rang as she shaved millimeters from the sponge cake. Her son, Robert, was excited. "Mum, I've got news." Libby's heart leapt. He was getting engaged at last. There would be a wedding. She'd need a new dress, and a hat...

"Are you listening? I've discovered a new great, great, great aunt, and what's more, she lived in Somerset." Libby sighed and cast a despairing glance at the meringue mixture she'd whipped to exactly the right consistency, as it collapsed, ruined.

When he was a studious, serious teenager, Robert preferred history to football and Latin to art. He encouraged Libby to join the local history society in Exham on Sea. "You'll meet some interesting people."

Libby had little interest in the Forest relations, Trevor's ancestors, but Robert worshipped his father. He never saw Trevor's dark side. She made an effort to sound interested. "Do tell me about it, darling."

"You know Dad always said his family were landowners?"

"Mm-hm." Did he? Libby swallowed a mouthful from a second cup of coffee. She added a slug of whisky and licked her lips.

"Well, I've found someone called Matilda Forest, and she's a maid in a Victorian house." Libby almost wished Trevor were here now. An ancestor in service: let him bluster his way out of that.

Robert was still talking. "And the house is in Somerset, near you. It's open to the public. Maybe we can all go and visit? Sarah's keen." Sarah was his girlfriend. Libby wasn't sure how long she'd stick with dull-but-worthy Robert.

Her interest sparked, she asked, "What did you find out about this Matilda?"

"Well, she had to leave the Hall because she was pregnant. She moved to the next village. The baby kept her surname, but, get this, Mum, his Christian names were Stephen Arthur, and those were the names of the Earl who lived in the house."

Libby chuckled. "Are you telling me, your father's ancestor was what they used to call, 'No better than she should be,' after hanky-panky with his lordship?"

"Honestly, Mum, Dad would be mortified."

"So he would."

The phone rang again. Still smiling, Libby picked it up. "Hello, darling, what did you forget?"

The deep voice on the other end of the phone brought her back to reality with a thud. "Is that Mrs Forest? It's Detective Sergeant Joe Ramshore here."

Libby let the silence draw on for a moment. She really didn't want to talk about the body under the lighthouse. She'd pushed Susie Bennett to the back of her mind. She let her breath out in a long sigh. "Yes, it's me."

"Well, I'm ringing to thank you for your help today." Joe Ramshore was the young detective from the beach. The one with blue eyes and a superior expression. "We wanted to let you know we've identified the lady you found."

"Susie Bennett?"

"Oh. You've heard, then." He sounded put out. "We think we know what happened, Mrs Forest. I thought you'd like to know that the deceased—" He coughed. "I mean, Susie Bennett, seems to have been alone when she died. I didn't want you to worry. It was all an unfortunate accident."

"An accident?" It didn't make sense.

The detective was still talking. "Yes, I'm afraid she had an awful lot to drink. We think she-er-vomited and choked. No one else involved. Only happened a few hours before you found her, though it's hard to tell the time of death, what with the cold water, and so on."

"Oh." What an anti-climax: to die like that, so foolishly. "What about the ring?"

"The ring?" He sounded puzzled. "Oh, yes, that bit of plastic on the sand. It was just a toy ring, nothing valuable. I expect it was in one of her pockets."

"But—" Libby broke off. No need to confess to moving the body. She compromised. "I just wondered why she'd have a plastic ring in her pocket."

"Oh, I see. Well, we don't know." The police officer's tone was measured, pedantic. "She wouldn't have been wearing it, would she? It's a child's ring."

Libby rolled her eyes. She could work that out without his help. "Yes, but—"

"We had a look at it, but there wasn't anything

we could use: no fingerprints or anything, I mean. The weather saw to that."

Libby insisted. "I meant, did Susie Bennett have a family?"

"Ah, I see what you're thinking. You're wondering if she has young children."

Libby, exasperated, crossed her eyes and waggled her head. Good thing the police officer couldn't see her. "Yes."

"I can put your mind at rest on that, Mrs Forest. We don't know of any family, as yet. Of course, we're getting records over from the US, because her husband was American."

"Yes, yes I heard that. You know, from people in the town."

"Well, it's a small town. I'll let you know when the inquest comes up. The coroner will want to ask you some questions. Nothing you need worry about. It's not like going to a criminal court."

"No, well, thank you."

"Try to put it out of your mind, Mrs Forest. I know it's upsetting, but these things do happen, I'm afraid."

Libby put the phone down. Too restless to go back to the spoiled meringue, she climbed the stairs to the bathroom. A hot bath might relax her.

She tried to unwind by reading a magazine, but her mind drifted away to the image of Susie

Bennett, drenched and cold, slipping sideways in dreadful slow motion. The scene played over and over in her head, like a YouTube video on a never-ending loop.

It was no good. She stepped out of the bath. How could she leave it at that? If the police weren't going to try to discover the truth, Libby would find out for herself. Was Susie's death really an accident, or something much worse?

CHAPTER FOUR

Fuzzy's Disgrace

The early morning sun peeped, pink and coy, over the horizon, as though the past two days of storms and wind belonged to another era. Libby walked Shipley along the beach in the opposite direction from the lighthouse. She wasn't ready to repeat yesterday's disastrous trip.

A dozen fishermen, with all the time in the world, leaned against the sea wall, rods extended into an ebbing tide. They nodded, mumbling a greeting as Libby passed. George Edwards wrapped a fish in newspaper. "For breakfast."

"How's your wife?"

"On the mend. The voice is back, more's the pity. By the way," he called Libby back. "She loved the cake. Keep a signed copy of your book back for me, will you? Do for her Christmas present." *Poor Mrs Edwards, was that going to be her only present?*

When she arrived home, Fuzzy, Libby's aloof marmalade cat, left the airing cupboard to follow her mistress into the kitchen, meowing pitifully. "Are you hungry, then?" Libby picked her up, nuzzling the soft, pale fur. Fuzzy allowed this display of affection for a count of three, then squirmed, squeaked and wriggled away. Libby opened a can of salmon.

Full, content and purring, Fuzzy left the house, via the cat flap in the back door. She'd work off breakfast chasing the mice, frogs and birds that had made the neglected garden their home, long before Libby moved in. "A wildlife garden," Libby explained, when Ali phoned. Her daughter had protested against Libby's crazy move from London to a quiet seaside town. "No need to weed the borders."

Libby downed a second mug of tea, shrugged on a bright red trench coat guaranteed to brighten her mood, and climbed into her tiny, eleven-year-old Citroen, to drive to work at the bakery.

Reversing out of the drive could be a challenge. The road she lived on wasn't exactly busy, for most traffic used the parallel main road, but it was ever-changing. Mums and Dads walked their children round the corner each day, heading for the nearby primary school. Teenagers, ears plugged with headphones, materialised suddenly from behind parked vans, mouths open in amazement at finding cars on the road.

It was too early for young people, today. They'd still be struggling awake. Libby switched on the ignition and reversed the car, hands light on the wheel, head turned to peer through the rear window.

A flurry of barking exploded nearby, like a pack of hounds after a fox. Libby jumped, foot jerking on the accelerator. The vehicle lurched. She jammed on the brake, but it was too late. The rear of the car crumpled with a sickening crunch, as it hit the lamppost on the corner.

Libby threw the door open, to find her exit blocked by a dog. It reached almost to her shoulder as it struggling on its lead, howling like a wolf. "Be quiet, Bear." The grey-haired man on the other end of the lead yanked the dog back, to let Libby out of the car. "Sit down."

The dog subsided, panting, saliva dribbling from its tongue. Libby slammed the door. "That animal should be locked up."

The man bent over the rear of the Citroen. "I'm afraid there's a dent."

"Of course there is. Your dog's a menace."

He straightened up, towering several inches above Libby. "He's not mine," he said. "I hope you're not hurt?"

Libby pointed. "Just look what you've done to my car."

"Forgive me, but you were driving. All Bear did was bark at that cat." Libby followed the pointing finger. Her shoulders slumped. Fuzzy crouched on top of the fence, fur fluffed out, laser-beam eyes trained on Bear. The dog, tantalised by a tormentor so close, yet out of range, howled again.

If a cat could be said to smirk, that's what Fuzzy did. Libby groaned. "Oh. That's my cat," she blurted. "Well, my husband's. Late husband." The back of her neck was hot. She tried to smile. "I'm afraid Fuzzy's nothing but trouble."

"Fuzzy?" The man grinned.

"Her fur goes Fuzzy in the rain."

"Well, I'm afraid there's not much we can do about the car. Your insurance will cover it." The stranger smiled, waved and went on his way. Bear barked once more, in a forlorn attempt to entice Fuzzy down from the fence.

Libby rubbed at the dent. The paint was intact and it was only a tiny bump. A garage would knock it out in minutes. She straightened up. That man could have apologised a bit more, though. Who was he? Where had he come from? She hadn't seen him before around here, but he looked familiar, nevertheless. She glared at Fuzzy. "Last salmon you'll get from me."

21

CHAPTER FIVE

The Bakery

Frank brought a tray of bread, steaming and fragrant, through into the bakery, just as Libby arrived. "Morning," he sang out. "What's the latest on Susie Bennett, then?" He scooped up a pile of baking trays, already on the way back to the kitchen. "They say her last album will be back in the charts, now she's dead. Too late for her, but it makes you wonder who'll get all those royalties."

The shop's work experience teenager leaned on the counter, twirling a stud on her lip. Libby secretly called her Mandy the Goth. "My Dad went to school with her."

Libby laughed. "So did half the town, I gather."

"I heard you found her. Was it gruesome? Was there much blood?" The girl's eyes, black with layers of kohl and mascara, were enormous in the white-painted face. Two silver rings decorated one nostril, above purple lips.

"Mandy." Frank put his head round the door. "Get on with those sandwiches before the rush starts. Wash your hands and put some gloves on."

22

Mandy sighed, rolled her eyes, hitched up a long, black lace skirt and went back to scraping egg mayonnaise into baguettes. "Dad said she was always asking for it," she muttered under her breath, glancing towards the kitchens. "Sexy but stupid, he said."

The bakery did a roaring trade. Almost everyone in town dropped in, keen to take a look at the person who found the body. Frank beamed. "That's the most sandwiches we've sold since Jeremy Clarkson came down, to drive off the pier."

By eleven o'clock, Libby's feet ached. Her head throbbed from the effort of repeating, "I just happened to find her," and, "The police say there's nothing suspicious." When the queue no longer snaked out of the door and round the corner, but had shrunk to one or two stragglers, she retreated to the kitchen. Mandy could serve the final few High Street estate agents.

Frank removed his white hat. "Can you finish that new ginger and lemon recipe by this afternoon, Libby? I reckon it'll be a winner."

"Mmm. Just need to tweak the frosting. A bit over-sweet, I thought."

"You're the expert. It'll sell like hot cakes." Libby grimaced. Frank made the same joke at least once a week. "Funny thing," he went on. "Millions

23

of people watch cooking programmes on TV, and half of 'em don't know how to turn on their ovens. Still, mustn't grumble. Where would the business be if everyone did their own baking, eh?"

Frank left to drive the van, loaded with filled rolls, to a nearby conference centre. Libby took a deep breath, drinking in the smell of fresh-baked bread. She tied on a clean apron, and set about testing the new recipe, relishing the familiar, satisfying tasks of measuring sugar, beating eggs and sifting flour. She'd have to persuade Frank to let her put the new confection in the book.

Mandy joined her. Libby opened her mouth to tell the teenager to stay in the shop, ready for new customers, but one look at the girl's face changed her mind. Mandy's lip trembled. Libby said, "We'll hear the bell if anyone comes."

Mandy grunted, tipped a bowl of risen dough onto a bench top and pummelled it. Libby watched. Nothing relieved angry feelings better than bread-making. It had been a favourite therapy during her miserable marriage.

For ten minutes, only Mandy's effortful gasps and the whirr of the food-processor disturbed the peace of the kitchen. The corners of Mandy's mouth still drooped. She sniffed. Libby had an idea. "Why don't you make the frosting?"

As Mandy dumped the bread dough back into a

stainless steel bowl, for its final proving, she explained. "I've weighed everything out, but the sugar needs watching." The teenager scraped dough from sticky fingers, shrugged and picked up a wooden spoon. "Make sure it all melts before you turn up the heat. That stops the mixture turning into a gritty mess."

Mandy, eyes on the saucepan, stirred. "Mrs Forest?"

"Mm-hmm." Best not to sound too interested.

"Dad threw a knife at Mum."

"A knife?" Libby stiffened, sugar spilling from the spoon. Her hand shook.

"It was only a knife from the table – not a carving knife or anything."

"Is your Mum OK?"

Mandy nodded. "Think so. She says it's not the first time, nor the last. He missed, anyway."

Libby lowered the spoon and took Mandy by the shoulders. "Your Mum needs to tell the police."

The girl shrugged Libby's hands away and swiped a sleeve across her eyes, smudging black mascara across one cheek.

"She won't. I've told her. She says he doesn't mean it."

"Mandy, that's rubbish." Libby closed her eyes, fighting memories. She took a long, slow breath.

25

"Of course he's sorry, afterwards. They always are, but it happens again." Fingernails bit into the palm of her hand. "Has he ever hit you?"

Mandy tossed her head. "He tells Mum it's her fault for making him angry, but anything sets him off. It was just about watching football on the telly, yesterday."

Libby pulled out a chair and eased on to it. She'd had just such a stupid row with Trevor. They argued—shouted—about nothing, and she threw his dinner in the bin. He cracked the TV remote control against her shoulder, all his strength behind the blow. His face, contorted with fury, sometimes appeared in Libby's dreams. She'd been terrified he'd hurt the children.

"Mandy." She took a moment to control her voice. "Mandy, if your mother won't do anything about it, then you should leave the house. You're old enough."

Mandy bent over the saucepan. "I think the sugar's ready to boil."

Libby handed over the sugar thermometer. "Think about it. I've got spare beds at my house if you need them."

Mandy sniffed and rubbed her nose, but said no more. Libby let it go. The girl had to make up her own mind.

The doorbell tinkled. Libby left Mandy at the

26

hob, watching water boil in the pan, and stepped into the shop, pulling on a pair of clean white gloves. "Can I help you?"

Tall, grey-haired, a little older than Libby, and dressed in a long blue overcoat, the new arrival smiled. "Good morning."

Libby stared. "It's you. The man with the dangerous dog."

"So it is. We seem to have got off to a bad start."

"I should say so."

He grinned. "I gave Bear a good talking to before I handed him back to Mrs Thomson."

Libby's lips twitched. "Quite right. He needs to learn to behave. Fuzzy's a bit of a menace, of course."

"Well, to be honest, I liked the look of Fuzzy. I admire a cat that stands up for itself. Bear doesn't agree."

Libby looked at the blue eyes. Yes, definitely familiar. Where else had she seen them? "Did you want a sandwich? Or cake?"

"Just a ham salad baguette, please." He patted his middle. "Have to watch the weight, these days."

Mandy arrived from the kitchen. She'd redone her mascara. "The frosting's ready, Libby." She stopped. "Hello, Mr Ramshore."

Libby looked from one to the other. "Ramshore. Like the detective sergeant?"

He smiled. "My son."

CHAPTER SIX

Coffee and Suspicion

This new Ramshore's first name turned out to be Max. "My parents were Norwegian." That explained the blue eyes.

Libby chose a table in a corner of the coffee shop, while he bought two lattes. "I thought I owed you a cup of coffee. I wasn't too gracious, earlier. Bear is much too big and loud."

"What breed is he?"

"Carpathian Sheepdog. Very gentle, like many big dogs, but he needs an incredible amount of exercise. He belongs to my neighbour, Mrs Thomson, really. Her husband kept him on the farm, but old Eric had to go into a care home before he died—dementia, I'm afraid. I bought the farm and I look after Bear when he gets too much for Mrs T. Which is quite often. She still lives in the old farmhouse down the lane from me."

"Well, anyway." Libby wasn't ready to forgive him, or Bear, completely. Besides, she was suspicious. "Did you know I worked at the bakery? I'm sure you didn't just happen to walk in today."

"No, to be honest, my son told me about you."

"The detective sergeant? What did he say?" She glared. "Aren't the police supposed to keep things confidential?"

"He just suggested I look out for you, on my marathon Bear-walk this morning. He thought you might be upset, after that business on the beach. Then, you had your little accident."

"Caused by Bear."

"And Fuzzy." His eyes twinkled. "I can see we're not going to agree on that. Anyway, I felt bad, so I asked one of your neighbours where you might be going. It's a small town, you know."

Where did looking out for each other stop and nosiness begin? "Have you always lived here?"

He nodded. "I went to school with Susie Bennett, you know. She wasn't in my year, she's a couple of years younger, but I knew her." Libby waited for the inevitable slur on Susie's character, but he surprised her. "She was a nice girl. Not such a nice family, though."

"Oh?" Libby hesitated. "You're the first person I've heard say anything good about her."

"Who have you asked? Wait. Let me guess. The WI?"

"No." Libby's face burned. "The local history society, actually. They all knew her at school."

30

"And didn't approve."

"Maybe they were jealous?" She was thinking aloud.

He stirred coffee with a long spoon. "Susie was too pretty for her own good, and too ready to believe everything the boys told her. You know how teenage boys can be. They try it on with girls, then if one says yes, they pull her reputation to pieces. That's how it was with Susie. Hardly any friends, just boys who wanted her for one thing. She had a terrific singing voice, though."

"I hear her album's going back on sale."

He crumbled a macaroon onto the table. "The vultures don't wait long to make a profit, do they?"

"She went to America, before she became famous, didn't she?"

"It all started here, though. Small local gigs at first. It was at Glastonbury, where they got their big break."

Libby shivered. "Glastonbury. Cold, wet and smelly, as I remember."

He laughed. "You've been there, then? Still, it's great place for up-and-coming bands. Mickey Garston, the big American music producer, heard Susie there, signed up the band and married her. It all happened pretty fast. He whisked her away and the next we knew, she was on the cover of million-selling albums and on TV."

"What about her family?"

"All dead or gone away. No Bennetts left in the town."

"That's sad."

"Typical story of a small-time girl with a turbulent life, I'm afraid. The marriage with Mickey Garston didn't last long. They split up years ago, but she never married again."

"No, she wasn't wearing a wedding ring when I found her." Did Max know about the plastic ring? Had Joe told him she'd moved the body?

Max drank the last drops of coffee and set the cup down with care. "My son mentioned a different ring. He said you seemed bothered by it."

"Bothered? No, why should I be?" Her face was burning.

"Come on. What are you hiding? I'm not the police, you know."

"No, but your son is." She bit her lip. Now it sounded as though she'd committed a huge crime. "OK. I moved the body. I pulled her hand out of her pocket and the ring fell on the beach. That's all. I know I shouldn't have touched her, but she looked so—well—vulnerable, I suppose. I wanted to help. Does that sound crazy?"

"I told you, I'm not the police." It was his turn to hesitate. "Truth is, I know a bit more about

Susie than the others around here. It's private information, and maybe I shouldn't tell anyone, but it makes me think there was something more going on than her committing suicide."

Libby licked dry lips. "D'you mean, you think she was murdered?"

"Mmm. Sounds a bit melodramatic, doesn't it?"

Libby thought about it. "That scene at the beach—it wasn't like a suicide."

"The police have closed the case, at least unless the coroner disagrees." He shook his head. "Frankly, if no one does anything, she'll be a statistic: just another girl who grew too rich and famous and couldn't handle it. I don't want to let that happen."

"What is it you know?"

Max blinked and looked away. "Not here. We need to talk somewhere more private. Can I take you to dinner tonight? There's a restaurant near Taunton where they know me. They'll let us have a quiet table."

Libby bit her lip. "All right." She stood up. "I've got to get back to the shop. Pick me up at seven?"

CHAPTER SEVEN

Dinner

Libby changed her dress three times before seven o'clock. It was stupid to feel so nervous. *I'm behaving like a teenager.* She hadn't been out alone with a man since Trevor died. The last thing she wanted was an entanglement. Not now, as she started to build the life she'd always wanted.

The linen shift dress was elegant, and a shade of pale rose that brought colour to her cheeks, but it creased too much, and anyway, the neckline was too low. She tossed it on the bed. This wasn't a date.

She tried a silk dress with a high waist and flared skirt that made her look girly. "Mutton dressed as lamb," she told Fuzzy, who rolled on the linen dress, covering it with ginger and white hairs.

Libby shooed the cat away and pulled out a pair of black evening trousers, matching them with a white shirt. There, that didn't give out any awkward signals. It was neat and business-like, but the trousers were well cut and the subtle embroidery, like damask, made them chic enough for evening. A silver chain round her neck, a heavy silver cuff on her wrist, and a squirt of scent completed her preparation, just in time. The bell rang as she left the room.

He was early. Libby ran downstairs, stomach fluttering, took a breath and opened the door. Mandy, hair wildly backcombed into an unruly bird's nest, rested a foot on the doorstep as if poised for retreat. In one hand, she hefted an unwieldy backpack with a black t-shirt spilling out of the top. The other hand was at her mouth, teeth tearing at a black-painted fingernail. She dropped the hand long enough to whisper, "Did you mean it? Can I really come to stay?"

"Of course you can stay." Mandy staggered into the hallway and Libby took the bag. "Good heavens, whatever have you got in there?"

Mandy made a sound halfway between a laugh and a sniff. "My laptop. And some books."

Books? Mandy? "Well, you're welcome to stay. Does your Mum know you're here?"

"I didn't tell her." Mandy's fingernail was back in her mouth. She looked like a frightened child.

"You should let her know. Won't she worry?"

"I'll ring her later. Dad won't be back tonight. He's going out drinking with his old mates and staying over at the Watson's place." Maybe

Samantha would keep an eye on Mandy's father: help him stay out of trouble. Libby would ask Max about Mandy's dad, this evening. He'd know what to do. His son was a police officer.

Mandy, gaining confidence once the front door closed, perched on a stool in the kitchen, gazing round the room, eyes wide. "Wow. What a place, Mrs Forest."

"Call me Libby. Now, I have to go out this evening, but the bed's made up in the spare room. I won't be late. Make yourself at home and help yourself to anything you can find."

Mandy was scooping walnut brownies from a tin when Max arrived. "Don't worry about me." She looked from Libby to Max and back, the hint of a smile on her face. She'd be on Facebook before Libby and Max were out of the drive. By tomorrow, everyone in town would know they'd been out for dinner.

Max drove a comfortable, well-used Range Rover. Bear lay in the back, greeting Libby with a bark. "Hello to you, too," she said, pulling his ears.

Max raised his eyebrows. "Hope you don't mind if Bear comes too. He likes the White House."

The restaurant was by the river, a string of tables lining the bank. There was an autumn chill. Good job she'd brought a jacket. Libby rejected

36

Max's polite invitation to eat inside. Bear made himself at home, disappearing into the reeds on the river bank, searching for a succession of sticks for Max to throw.

"If you grew up in Exham, you must know just about everybody in town." Libby had spent all her life, until now, in West London. "I meet a new person one day, like Mandy at the bakery, and next day I drop into the newsagent and find her mother works there. It's like a spider's web."

"It's useful. If you need a job done, you can always find a friend or relative of someone you know, who can help."

"I need someone to renovate my bathroom. Any ideas?"

He tapped his fingers on the table. "There's always Bert, that's Mandy's Dad, if you want it done for cash, with no questions asked. But I wouldn't advise that. A bit crooked, is Bert. Try Ned Watson. He does building and plumbing. Tell him I sent you, and he'll give you a decent price. We were at school together."

"Tell me more about Mandy's father."

Max grimaced. "The man's a bully. He was like it at school. No one's lunch money was safe."

Libby peeked at Max's shoulders, broad as a boxer's. Her lips twitched. "I bet yours was."

He smiled. "I can look after myself. Since

37

school, Bert's been on the dole most of the time, though he makes plenty by cleaning windows: cash payments only, of course."

"Is Mandy's mother safe? Won't he hurt her?"

Max took a sip of ice-cold Pinot Grigio. "I'm not sure. Bert goes down the pub with a bunch of his loser pals, gets drunk and takes it out on Elaine. The police are called round there from time to time." He shrugged. "Usual story. Wife takes him back every time. Refuses to press charges. She's had a black eye or two." Max's own eyes glinted, cold as ice. "I try to keep an eye out for Elaine. Bert listens to me, so long as he's sober. We go back a long way, but I'm not always successful. One day, he'll go too far."

Libby swallowed. "Well, she'll be OK tonight. He's staying with the Watsons."

Max laughed. "Samantha must be away. She'd never let Bert stay if she was at home. She rules Ned with a rod of iron."

"Anyway, Mandy's safe with me. Her father won't even know she's there."

"He'll hear soon enough: you can't keep secrets in Exham on Sea, you know." Max topped up her glass. "Don't worry about Mandy. She's eighteen, old enough to make her own decisions."

He swished wine around his glass. "What about you? How did you get here?"

"My husband died."

"I'm sorry."

She met his eye. "Don't be. I'm not." His eyebrows shot up. Libby laughed. "Sounds dreadful, I know, but he was my big mistake. My parents warned me." She hadn't listened, and she'd never told them they were right. "I know it sounds awful, but when Trevor had a heart attack, I cheered inside. At last, I could work, have my own life, make friends and live where I chose. I chose Exham on Sea." She raised her glass. "To my new life."

"Now," she put the menu to one side. "We didn't come here to talk about me. Tell me about Susie Bennett."

CHAPTER EIGHT

Nest Egg

Max drummed his fingers on the table. "The thing is, Susie kept in touch after she left. I used to live and work in Bath, in one of the banks, and Susie came in one day, before she left for America, and opened an account."

"Was she rich?"

"Not rich, then, though she was later, but I don't think she ever trusted Mickey. I tried to stop her going away with him." Max's eyes were focused on his plate. Did he still hold some sort of a candle for Susie? It would explain why he was the only person in Exham on Sea with a good word to say for her. "She wouldn't listen. Said she could handle herself, but wanted to be sure there were funds somewhere safe, that only she knew about, in case she, or anyone else, ever needed them."

Their steak arrived, and Max stopped talking, refilling Libby's glass with red wine and taking a deep draught from his own. Libby sliced into her food, watching blood trickle from the rare steak.

"Or anyone else," she murmured. "What could she have meant by that?"

Max shrugged. "She wouldn't say. Just told me it was her secret and she'd let me know when she wanted the money. That's all there is to it."

"That's all?"

"I shouldn't even be telling you." The sharp edge was back in his voice.

Libby ignored it. "I'm glad you did. What happens to the money now?"

"There's been a pretty big pot waiting for Susie, but she never used it. Never came back, just contacted me from time to time, to check on the interest. In the early years, we spoke about every six months. She talked about needing it soon, but after a while, she stopped contacting me."

"When was that?"

"Oh, six or seven years after she married. About the time of her last album. You remember, Twilight over the Sea?"

Libby did remember. Susie's dark contralto voice blending with a plaintive guitar in sad songs of love and loss. Her best work, the critics said. "She never made another album, did she?"

"No, that was it. She lived the rock and roll lifestyle with Mickey: plenty of drugs and booze. They broke up a few years later, and she wrote to me again, asking me to keep the account open. She said she'd probably not need it, anyway. That was the last time we were in contact, apart from the statements sent by the bank."

Libby took a chance. "You were pretty close to Susie, then, if she trusted you with her money?"

His eyes narrowed. "What gossip have you been listening to?"

Libby held his gaze, keeping her voice steady. "I don't listen to gossip, but you're the only one I've met so far who knew Susie after she left." Max twirled a spoon in his fingers. His eyes slid away, looking out over the hills. Libby pulled her jacket more tightly round her shoulders.

"Susie and I had a business relationship. It was no more than that."

"But you'd have liked it to be more?"

Max's eyes narrowed. Libby flinched at the steely undertone to his voice. "It's none of your business, Mrs Forest."

She gripped her hands under the table. She murmured, "Did your wife know how you felt about Susie?"

Max's eyes were stony. "We're divorced."

"Because of Susie?"

He laughed, suddenly, and drained his glass with a flourish. "Oh, Mrs Forest, how very inquisitive you are. Do you think I murdered Susie Bennett?"

42

"I don't know, but I'm sure someone killed her. I'm just trying to find out more about the people who knew her. You're one of them. I thought you wanted to help."

The anger died from his face. "Of course I do. Well, you'll have to make up your own mind about me, but for what it's worth, I didn't kill Susie, even though I was no model husband. To answer your question, Susie was just one of the reasons my wife and I quarrelled. But there were plenty of others. Now, if you've had enough to eat, we'd better move inside. The wind's getting up."

Sure enough, a gust of wind blew napkins from the table and raindrops splattered the cloth. Max rose to his feet, calling Bear back from the river. The dog arrived, wet, muddy and smelly. Libby shivered. "Maybe we'd better just leave?"

CHAPTER NINE

Walnut brownies

Max drew up behind the Citroen. "You'd better get that dent fixed. Try Jenkins' Garage, it's the best around this area."

"I suppose you were at school with Mr Jenkins."

"As it happens, I was."

"Another member of The Band of Brothers?"

Max put the car into gear as Libby climbed out. "I suppose you could call it that. We look out for each other."

The house lay quiet, the kitchen clean and tidy. Mandy was on her best behaviour. How long would it last? Libby fell into bed, stomach full of good food and wine, and slept heavily until morning.

The phone startled her awake. "I've been thinking about that money of Susie's." Max didn't bother to ask how she was. This relationship was strictly business. Libby yawned and focused on his voice. "Anything she saved will be part of her estate and go to her heirs. I'm wondering who they

44

might be."

The smell of burnt toast and the sound of scraping rose from the kitchen, and Libby's mouth watered. She tried to concentrate as Max talked. "I'm going over to the States. I've got Susie's old address. I think we need to let people know what's happened."

"Isn't that a police job?"

"No, not if there's no foul play in the case, apparently, and no grieving husband or children. Someone needs to find a solicitor, or attorney, or whatever they're called in the US, and sort out wills and so on."

"So, you're going to do it."

"Er—yes. Well, there's no one else, is there? It'll take ages if we wait until after the inquest and anyway..."

He let the words hang in the air, but Libby knew what he was thinking. Justice for Susie. "I'm off to Heathrow now. There's a flight this afternoon."

"Already? What about Bear? Who's going to walk him?" *Shut up, Libby, what are you saying?*

"I've left him with Mrs Thomson. He'll have to wait for his exercise until I get back."

Libby let the silence grow. It wasn't her job to look after that huge dog. She groaned. "I'll go and rescue him. I don't see why he has to suffer."

45

"Libby, you're a treasure."

"I am. You'd better tell me anything you find out. And Max, there's one question we have to answer."

"What's that?"

"If she's been living in the US since the 1990s, with no contact with anyone in England, what the heck was she doing on Tuesday on the beach at Exham on Sea?

She put the phone down. *And why are you so keen to go to the States? What are you up to?*

She rang Ned Watson, mentioned Max's name and asked him to give a quote for the bathroom. He was business-like. "I like a week, to do a bathroom. You don't want to rush it." He'd come round tomorrow. Libby, used to long waiting lists for any work in London, was impressed. She couldn't wait to see the back of the orange tiles and avocado green bath.

***

Mrs Thomson's old, tumbledown house lay just outside town, surrounded on three sides by green fields, cattle and a green knoll that rose in a rounded hump from the Somerset levels. A flock of sheep speckled the slopes, along with three or four horses.

Libby peered up the lane. A few stray leaves, hardy enough to withstand the gales, still clung to the branches of a row of trees—horse chestnuts, perhaps. The tracery of branches framed a neat, white-painted building. That must be Max's place. Libby whistled. Max Ramshore lived in style. *Mr Lord of the Manor.*

What was it he did, exactly, that he could desert at such short notice to go to the states? He'd left the bank, but he was way off retirement age. Or, was he going to America for some other reason, using Susie as an excuse?

Beyond Mrs Thomas' house, dunes led down towards the golf club and beach. The nine-legged lighthouse must be nearby. Libby dragged on the brake, eased out of the car, tugged the battered boot until it opened with a screech, and rescued a box of walnut brownies. Tucking it under one arm, she scanned the net curtains for signs of occupancy.

She thumbed the doorbell and waited. No answer. She rapped on the wood of the door, and leaned harder on the bell. No one in. Maybe she'd do some snooping round Max's house. As she stepped back, Bear bounded round the corner, greeting her with the enthusiasm of a long lost friend. With a super-human effort, she kept her feet, pushing the dog's wet nose away from her face. The door creaked open.

An aged head appeared in the gap between

door and lintel, hearing aid just in sight behind each ear. Libby recognised the old lady's Victory Roll hairstyle, popular at the end of the Second World War. Her great aunt used to wear one. "Mrs Thomson?" Libby raised her voice. Deafness must be a blessing to anyone who lived with Bear and his ear-splitting bark, but it was going to make conversation difficult.

The lady of the house screwed up her eyes and squinted. "Are you the dog-walker for Bear?"

So far, so good. "Max Ramshore sent me. He said you'd like me to come and help with Bear while he's away. I've brought some brownies."

The door closed. A chain rattled and Mrs Thomson pushed the door wide, beckoning with one hand as she untied her apron with the other. "Come on, come in. I'll make a cup of coffee and see if we've got any biscuits. You must be hungry, coming all this way." She led Libby through the house, talking all the time.

All this way? From Exham? "I've brought brownies," she repeated.

"Yes, we get a lot of townies here. They like to walk on the Knoll."

CHAPTER TEN

Annie Rose

Mrs Thomson's long, low sitting room looked out over the dunes. The windows were small and wooden, long overdue an update to double glazing. Libby shivered. The wind from the sea must blow straight through the crumbling wood. She could smell the salt from here.

Mrs Thomson shook her head at Libby's bawled offer of help in the kitchen, pointed to the sofa and went out. Libby tried to remove dog hairs from the tapestry cushions decorating the sofa, changed her mind about sitting down, and stepped over to the window. It took an effort of will to make herself look right, along the beach to the lighthouse.

The tide was out again, leaving the building's stumpy legs exposed in the mud. Libby released her breath in a relieved sigh. No body today.

Mrs Thomson returned, balancing a tray painted with cats. China cups and jugs rattled, as she lowered it to one of the side tables. Vases, silver-framed photos and dog-shaped ornaments teetered on the piano. Pictures of Bear, standing alongside a bent, aging man, hung on the walls. Mr Thomson?

His widow poured coffee and brought a cup to Libby at the window. "We've got three lighthouses in Exham, you know."

"Three?" Libby sipped the hot coffee.

"Yes." Mrs Thomson ticked them off on knobbly, arthritic fingers. "There's one on the beach, up there," she nodded to the right. "That's where they found Suzanne, the other day." Libby set her cup and saucer down on the table nearest to the hairy sofa and sat. She could brush her jeans later.

Mrs Thomson took a brownie. "These are nice, dear. Did you make them yourself?" She must have forgotten about the other two lighthouses.

Libby smiled. "You've heard about Susie Bennett, then, Mrs Thomson?"

Her companion shook her head, her brow folded into a criss-cross of lines. She looked about to burst into tears. "Oh, yes. Such a shame, a lovely girl like Suzanne."

Libby bit her lip. Mrs Thomson was old and widowed. Maybe asking questions, getting her to relive the past, would be cruel. Before she could decide, Mrs Thomson was talking. "I knew her before she was famous, when she was little girl, singing at the Christmas parties the vicar used to put on over there."

She pointed through the window to a small, squat church that lay almost on the dunes. "Suzanne, we called her, of course. I don't hold with shortening names that were given at a proper Christian baptism. The young people do it all the time, these days. You never know who's who. My name's Marjorie, and I never let anyone call me anything different, not even my Eric."

"Did you know Suzanne well?" Libby steered the conversation back to the past.

"My Eric used to play the piano while Suzanne sang. Such a pretty little thing, she was, all curls and a big smile." There were tears in the old lady's eyes.

What had she thought when Susie grew up and developed a taste for boys and fast living? "Did other children go to the parties, too?"

"All the boys and girls were there. There'd be dancing and games, Suzanne would sing and Maxwell would play the saxophone. You know Maxwell, don't you? Calls himself Max, nowadays. Of course you do. It's Maxwell sent you round to walk Bear." She leaned on the arm of the chair, pushing down for support and staggering to her feet. "I'm getting forgetful, that's my trouble. Where did I put Bear's lead, now?"

51

Libby cut in. "Please tell me more about Suzanne."

Mrs Thomson narrowed her eyes. "Why do you want to know about her? From the press, are you?" She pursed thin lips. "I know the girls from the local paper. You're not one of them. Are you from the Western Daily Press?" Her voice rose. "Anyway, I've nothing to say to you, so you'd better be getting off."

CHAPTER ELEVEN

Photographs

Judging by the unhealthy, deep red in Mrs Thomson's face, the elderly lady could be on the verge of a stroke. Libby held out her hands. "No, no. I'm not a reporter. It's just that—well, I found Susie's body, Mrs Thomson. Suzanne's, I mean. I was walking my friend's dog on the beach."

"Hm." Mrs Thomson stopped in mid-gesture. She stared hard at Libby, suspicious. Satisfied, she sank back into the chair, the livid colour slowly ebbing from her face. "I suppose Maxwell wouldn't have sent you round here if you were with the papers. He has his faults, that one, but at least his heart's in the right place."

Libby hesitated. She didn't want to risk hurting the old lady, but she needed to know more about Susie. "You must have been proud of Suzanne?"

"Mr Thomson used to keep all the cuttings from the newspapers, when she went to the States. Who'd have thought little Suzanne would make such a big name for herself?"

Libby took a shot in the dark. "Did she keep in

touch after she left Exham?"

"Oh yes, she used to send me all her records. Albums, they call them nowadays, of course. She sent a card at Christmas, as well, every year, regular as clockwork. All except for that one year."

"Which one was that?"

"The year the little girl died. It must have been, let me see, the little girl was seven, so that was back in the early 90s. She wrote and told me about it, but no cards that year. Not surprising. Poor Suzanne, it broke her heart."

Coffee scalded Libby's throat. "Little girl? She had a daughter?"

"Oh yes, she had a daughter in America. With Mickey what's-his-name. Big record executive, he was, or some such. Annie: that was the little girl's name. Annie Rose. Pretty little thing, she was, just like her mother. Here, wait, I've got a photo, somewhere."

Drawers opened and closed in another room. Mrs Thomson returned, clutching a red photo album, old green slippers soundless on the patterned carpet. Libby shifted along on the sofa, making room. Heads together, they flipped through pages of photos: babies, houses, older children. "Here we are." Mrs Thomson pointed at four photos behind a filmy, plastic sheet.

A neat, handwritten date and caption

54

accompanied every image. "My Eric put all our photos in an album, labelled and everything. He was like that. Always neat and tidy." Mrs Thomson peered round the room, maybe half-hoping to see the late Mr Thomson in his usual chair. "The farm was the best in the county. Our Herefords won prizes." Her shoulders slumped. She sighed, misty-eyed. "All sold, now."

Afraid the old lady was slipping into reminiscence about the farm, Libby tapped a finger on the photo at the top left of the page. "Is this Suzanne?"

"That's her. Still at school, then." Libby caught her breath, shocked to see a young Susie smiling in the photo, very much alive. Under the lighthouse, she'd been wet, bedraggled and dead. Nevertheless, this was the same person, no question. There was no mistaking the neat nose and arched eyebrows.

Mrs Thomson moved on to the other pictures. "Here she is, on stage in America." Two tall youths, one bowing a violin, the other behind a keyboard, each young face taut with concentration, dwarfed the singer. Despite her tiny stature, Susie's personality sprang from the photograph. She glowed, alive with the joy of performance, an enormous guitar slung round her long, white neck.

"This one's her wedding photo." Mrs

Thomson's voice jerked Libby back to the present. "And this—" one gnarled finger touched the last photograph, light as a caress, "is little Annie Rose."

Libby let her eyes slide down to the image of Susie's little girl. The child was a miniature of her mother. Hair so fair it was almost white, she struck a dancer's pose, toes pointed, arms in the air, delicate in a tiny version of her mother's fringed skirt and full-sleeved blouse.

Libby dragged her gaze from the dead child's enchanting dimples, and looked at the wedding photo. So, that was Mickey. He loomed over Susie, heavy arm pulling her off balance, crumpling the puffed satin wedding dress. The bride gazed up at her new husband, adoring, while he smirked at the camera, stealing the moment like a spoilt child.

Still, being self-centred and arrogant didn't mean he was responsible for Susie's lonely death. If Mickey was in Los Angeles on the day she died, he couldn't have killed her. Libby hoped Max would take a good look at the man's alibi. "Mrs Thomson, do you know how Annie Rose died?"

"Oh, dear. I'm afraid the poor thing drowned."

Libby's head spun. Perhaps Mrs Thomson was confused. "No, I mean Annie Rose, not Suzanne."

"That's right. She fell in the swimming pool." Mrs Thomson's eyes were very bright. "They all

56

have swimming pools, out in California. It's so hot, you see. It broke Suzanne's heart." Her smile trembled. "We never had children, Eric and me. Suzanne was like a daughter. We'd been so happy for her, with her little girl, doing so well. Then, Annie Rose died. It was quite dreadful. Eric never got over it."

Libby's stomach lurched. Had she jumped to conclusions? Maybe Susie had drowned herself, after all, still heartbroken, choosing to end her life as Annie Rose lost hers. Perhaps the police were right. She struggled for words. "How did you find out?"

"They rang, from America. Mickey's secretary, I think it was, said Suzanne was too upset to talk but she wanted us to know." Mrs Thomson took out a tiny white handkerchief and wiped her eyes. "There, it still upsets me, dear. I'm sorry to make a fuss. You see, it all happened so far away. And now this…" She blew her nose again, pocketing the scrap of cotton. "Well, these things happen. I'll make more coffee."

Mrs Thomson clattered in the kitchen. Libby flipped backwards through the pages of the album. She found a photo of a Christmas tree, piles of presents and rows of kids. They were about eleven or twelve years old, Libby guessed. The vicar beamed in the centre of the back row. She looked

57

closer. There was Susie—Suzanne—in the front row, a brace running along her teeth.

The tall, gangly boy standing beside Susie looked familiar. Yes. It was Max. Mrs Thomson returned, tray in hand, and leaned over Libby. "Look, there they all are. Most are still here, or hereabouts. There's Maxwell, of course, and Benedict who's married to Samantha. The one with the broken tooth is Alan - Alan Jenkins. Oh, look, there's Angela…"

She broke off as the doorbell rang. Libby jumped to her feet, glad of an excuse to avoid more coffee. Her insides were close to exploding. "Don't worry, Mrs Thomson. I'll open the door."

An elderly woman on the doorstep wrinkled her forehead, perplexed to find an unexpected stranger in her friend's house. "Oh. Is Regina in?" A cake-shaped parcel, wrapped in tin foil, peeped from her basket. Libby ushered the newcomer in, made her excuses to Mrs Thomson, grabbed Bear's lead and left them to their memories.

CHAPTER TWELVE

Bear Walk

Libby gripped Bear's collar, hauling him back as she unlocked the door. The last thing she needed was a confrontation with the cat. She shouted for Fuzzy, but as usual there was no response. That animal came only when she chose. She could be anywhere. Libby wasn't about to leave Bear outside, digging up the tiny garden. She wanted that dog where she could see him.

She shut the door to the sitting room. He wasn't going in there, either. She took him into the kitchen. Maybe he needed feeding. What did dogs eat? *Meat.* There was beef in the fridge. A treat for the weekend. Reluctant, she cut it up and dropped it in an old bowl. Bear leaped on it with enthusiasm. Libby filled another bowl with water and set it down near the food.

The builder, Samantha's husband, arrived, built like a footballer. He considered the bathroom. "These avocado suites were put in during the 70s," he said. "Don't see them around very often, these days." He laughed, twinkling at Libby.

59

She grinned back. "I can't wait to get rid of the tiles."

"It'll take me a week," he announced, once he'd measured the room. "I'll email the quote." He swallowed Libby's last brownie in one bite, and left.

Head teeming with plans for her spa bathroom, Libby climbed the stairs to the study, opened her laptop and pulled up a list of a hundred and twenty emails. Most were junk. A long page from her daughter tempted her, but she moved on. Ali would ring if there was a problem. This was a news bulletin. She'd enjoy it later.

Ah, there it was. Max had checked in, as promised. *Staying in luxury in Hollywood,* he gloated. *Contacted Mickey's company and got an appointment to see him this afternoon. Told them I was an old friend of Susie's and it was personal and urgent. Will let you know what happens.*

Libby snorted. Luxury in Hollywood would mean five star glamour. Flowers in the room, champagne on ice. Libby's family holidays had been camping in Scotland or a week in a chilly holiday cottage or, when the kids were teenagers, caravan holidays in France. Trevor never wasted money.

Libby closed the laptop, retrieved Bear from the kitchen, wiped up the water he'd splashed on the floor and set off, anorak hood firmly in place against the weather. The wind and rain grew stronger every moment. It was going to be a rough afternoon, and probably a stormy night. Summer seemed a very long time ago.

She turned away from the beach, heading for the fields, hoping Bear didn't chase sheep. Once there, she found a stick and threw it. Bear charged away, fur flying, grasped it in his teeth with hardly a pause, raced back and laid it triumphantly at her feet. Libby laughed aloud, pulled his ears and threw the stick again. Fuzzy would never dream of such undignified behaviour.

"Oi. You." The voice came from behind. "What the devil d'you think you're doing?"

A short, squat man wearing a waxed jacket and flat cap appeared at Libby's side. "We're not doing any harm." How dare he shout at her? This was a public footpath.

Oh. No. Now Libby thought about it, she realised it wasn't. She'd left the path some way behind. Still, there weren't any crops here to be trampled, and no sheep or cows. She'd brazen it out. The man's face was very red, his nose enormous and lumpy. *Drinks too much.*

"That dog's not on a lead. I could shoot him." The man's eyes were small. He narrowed them into angry slits.

"You haven't got a gun."

"Didn't say I was gonna shoot, did I? But I could."

They summed each other up. Libby stood as tall as her five foot four inches allowed and glared, hiding triumph as the man's gaze dropped. "What you doin' with Bear?"

"You know him, then?"

"Yeah, 'course I know him." He called out, "Hey, Bear." The dog raced over to lick his hand, happy to transfer his allegiance from Libby.

"Oh. Well, I'm walking him for Max."

"Ah. Max." He drew the word out. The grin was insulting. "Friend of yours, is he?"

"Not really. I'm a dog-walker. I'm just helping out Mrs Thomson while Max is away."

The man nodded, the smile even broader. "Gone far, has he?"

About to tell him to mind his own business, Libby stopped. Instead, she tried her best smile, head on one side, eyelashes fluttering. "He's very busy. I've no idea what he does all the time."

The man laughed. "Max has his fingers poking into all sorts of pies. You be careful, now, a nice lady like you." His eyes travelled up and down Libby's body.

Glad of the shapeless anorak, Libby tried another tack. "Do you live around here?"

"Over yonder, t'other side of the hill. Want to come and see?"

"Why not?" Was she mad? Libby straightened her shoulders. She could look after herself.

They trudged along the lane without speaking. He was definitely the strong, silent type. They turned the corner, but there was no sign of a house. The edge of the village began a hundred yards down the road, and the nearest building bore a garish sign, "Jenkins Garage." Libby's spirits rose, despite the missing apostrophe. That was the garage Max had mentioned. "Is that yours?"

"Yep. Alan Jenkins at your service, Ma'am." There was grime under his nails and oil stains on his coat. Not a farmer, after all. He'd been stringing her along. Libby wouldn't make much of a Sherlock Holmes. She hadn't recognised him as one of the boys in Mrs Thomson's photo album. Twenty years made a big difference.

Still, he might be a useful source of information. "Maybe you can help me. There's a dent in the back of my car."

"Jag, is it?"

"I wish. Citroen."

"You bring it round, I'll see what I can do."

Libby took Bear back to the house. She checked on Fuzzy in the airing cupboard, shut the dog in the kitchen, keeping a secure door between the two animals, and took the car round to Alan Jenkins at the garage.

He sucked his teeth. Libby rolled her eyes. He was ramping up the bad news so he could overcharge her. "Tell you what."

"Yes?" She braced herself.

"Seeing as you're a friend of Max's, I'll do it for nothing."

"What? Don't be ridiculous. Why would you do that?"

He sucked his teeth once more. "The thing is, Mrs-er…"

"Mrs Forest."

"Mrs Forest. The thing is, I owe Max a favour, just at the minute. I reckon, seeing as you and he are good friends, like, this 'ere'll pay it off."

Libby's blush rose hotly up her neck. "We're not good friends. I hardly know him."

"You were out at the White House t'other night, and that's a fact."

"Yes, but…" Libby's words tailed into silence as her brain raced. "Well, maybe we are friends. Max has plenty of friends."

"Yes, and I wouldn't want to be on the wrong side of most of 'em."

Libby swallowed. "So, what's the favour you owe him?"

"Now, that would be saying."

The man was putting on a good local yokel act, Libby had to hand it to him. "Come on, Mr—er—Alan. If you want me to help you get on the right side of Max, you'd better tell me a bit more, or else I'll give you a cheque and tell him you threatened me."

"I never did."

"I know that, but Max doesn't." Libby coughed, fighting a snort of laughter. Alan Jenkins had turned pale.

"All right." He looked around, to check they were alone. "There's been some ringing."

Libby tried to look intelligent. "Ringing? With—er—um…"

"Broken-down cars fit only for scrap, sold for next to nothing, tarted up, clock turned back, sold on to nice unsuspecting ladies, like you."

Together, they eyed Libby's car. "It came from a proper Citroen garage, I'll have you know."

He wiped his hands on the front of his overall. "Anyway, the garage got in a bit of trouble with a Bristol gang and Max—well, he sorted it out for me." Max had enough clout to scare off a gang of criminals, had he? Alan Jenkins picked up an oily rag and polished the wing mirrors of a small Renault. If Libby wanted to know more, it appeared she'd have to ask Max.

65

CHAPTER THIRTEEN

Mangotsfield Hall

"Where are you?"

"What?" The harsh trill of the phone broke into Libby's confused dream of sand, mud and dogs. "What time is it?"

Marina exhaled loudly. "It's half past one, and we're all here, waiting for you."

Libby shook her head, to click it into gear. "I fell asleep." She never fell asleep after lunch. She wished she'd kept Bear here, instead of walking him back to Mrs Thomson's house. He would have kept her awake. "I'm on my way."

Her heart sank. Today, the local history society was giving a talk about Victorian women at Mangotsfield Hall, the huge mansion nearby, owned by the National Trust. It was the place Robert mentioned. Trevor's ancestor had worked there as a maid.

In a rash moment, Libby had promised to let Marina use her as a model in a talk about costume. She'd forgotten about it. "You might have reminded me."

"We talked about it on Tuesday." Marina dropped the outraged voice. "Look, don't panic. Angela's doing the magic lantern show first, so you've got a bit of time. I know how you feel, I've been all of a tizz ever since the Susie thing. Just get here, as fast as you can."

"What about the refreshments?" Libby was supposed to have taken them across from the bakery this morning.

"Mandy brought them over. She said she stayed with you last night?" The question hung in the air. No problem with Marina's gossip antennae.

Libby ignored it. "Look, my car's in the garage. Can someone pick me up? I'll be ready in ten minutes."

She grimaced. She'd agreed to some crazy things, since she came to Exham, hoping to fit in with the townspeople, but it would probably take at least twenty years to be accepted as a local. She really ought to spend more time on her career. She was getting behind with the book, and it was time she booked another cooking course. Patisserie. That would be her future. Or maybe, chocolate. She'd see what Ali thought. She ran downstairs. Better not keep Marina waiting.

***

Marina's car screeched to a halt at the back of the Hall, at the tradesman's entrance. Libby

67

dashed through the sudden downpour, frantically grasping the edges of an umbrella as the wind threatened to turn it inside out. She pasted a serene expression on her face as they walked in. "It's OK." Marina poked her head through a crack in the door. "Angela's kept them busy." Laughter blared from the hall, followed by applause as Angela finished. "Come on, then," Marina hissed. "It's us next." She gave her friend a hearty shove and Libby half-fell into the hall.

She was never going to volunteer for anything, ever again. She really, really hated people staring. What had she been thinking? Well, too late now. She smiled through clenched teeth, lips stiff, as Marina dressed her up in Victorian costume and make-up, beginning with a cotton shift and working up through layers of corsets and wire crinoline cages. She wouldn't be able to bear the weight for more than five minutes. How did Victorian ladies keep going all day?

Marina attached false ringlets to the sides of Libby's head. "The Victorians thought it impolite for a lady to show her ears," she explained, taking a pot of strong-smelling potion and a paint brush, and smoothing oil over Libby's hair. As it dried, Libby shook her head, but the ringlets stayed rigidly in place.

The result was a passable imitation of Queen

Victoria. As though that were not sufficient humiliation, the audience gathered round, taking photos that threatened to haunt Libby for the rest of her life. They plucked at the costume, lifting heavy layers and letting them fall. "Look, you can hardly raise your arms, those sleeves are so tight."

"It's all part of the Victorian way of life," Marina said. "In fact, wearing a corset supports your back, don't you think, Libby,"

"I could wear this every day," Libby lied. "For one thing, it hides my waist. I could put on pounds and no one would notice."

Slowly, the audience dispersed, chattering happily. At last, she could get rid of the costume and have a few words with Marina. "What's in that disgusting stuff you spread all over my hair? You didn't warn me about that. How am I going to get it off?"

The words dried up on her lips as Libby caught sight of Detective Sergeant Joe Ramshore. She shifted, embarrassed. Did Joe know she'd been out to dinner with his father? Oh, well, who cared? She was a grown woman and Max was divorced. It was none of his son's business.

"Mrs Forest, I'm glad to see you." Joe focused on Libby's hair and smirked. "So sorry I missed the meeting. That costume looks terrific. And the hair…" He made a noise halfway between a laugh and a cough. "Actually, I'm one of the trustees of Mangotsfield Hall and it's my day off today, but I'd like to have a word with you."

Libby swallowed. Was she in trouble? About to be accused of obstructing the police by moving the body, and taken into custody? "Of course."

"I wanted to tell you we've had the pathologist's report. It's no more than we expected. The cause of death was drowning while intoxicated. He found alcohol and drugs in Susie's blood. Not a deliberate overdose, just enough to stop Susie taking proper care around the water."

"No sign of anything else?"

"A bruise on her head, but that would be the tide bashing her against the lighthouse. It was a rough old storm on Monday night."

Libby tried to think. "What about the time of death?"

"It's hard to tell. The body was in the water for a few hours, but it was so cold the pathologist can't tell when rigor mortis set in." Libby winced. It was the stiffness of rigor mortis that had kept Susie's hand in her pocket, until Libby pulled it out to point at the sky.

"Look, Detective—"

"Call me Joe."

"Look, aren't you going to investigate further? I mean, you said she was bruised. Don't you think that's suspicious? What if someone else was there?"

Joe sighed, looking suddenly tired. "Please, Mrs Forest. We're grateful to you for calling us in as soon as you found the body, but now, you must leave it to us. We've seen hundreds of accidental deaths, you know, especially when there's drink and drugs involved."

The patronising tone infuriated Libby. "I know that, but common sense—"

"Common sense tells us there was nothing suspicious." He'd raised his voice. "Now, let me give you a bit of advice." Joe's mouth smiled, but the eyes, so like his father's, told a different story. Libby resisted a shiver. "You're new here. You didn't know Susie. People feel strongly about her, around here. They're proud. Not many from Exham end up famous. Folk don't like anyone suggesting she's more than just unlucky."

The blue gaze bored into Libby. "We need to keep everyone calm. Talk a bit less about the drink and drugs, if you see what I mean. It was just an unfortunate accident." His tone was reasonable. "Walking on the beach at this time of year is dangerous. The sea comes in fast. Susie's been away a long time and she forgot about the power of the tide." He leaned towards Libby and spoke with emphasis. "It was an accident, Mrs Forest.

71

Leave it be. No more gossip."

Gossip? That was rich. The whole town was abuzz with scandal. Libby shrugged. "I didn't know her. I just found the body." She hoped he hadn't heard details of her conversations with Max or her visit to Mrs Thomson.

"Exactly. You didn't know her. I'm just saying, some folks here don't take kindly to a stranger, who wasn't here in the old days, stirring things up." His words silenced Libby. She tried to think of a sufficiently cutting reply, but before she could gather her wits, Joe walked away, leaving Libby, arms akimbo, mouth open.

Marina took her elbow. "Are you OK?"

"I don't know. I think I've just been told to keep my nose out of town affairs."

"By Detective Sergeant Joe?" Libby nodded. Marina waved a hand. "Don't worry about him. He can't get over his father coming back to town, just when Joe's been promoted to Chief Inspector's bagman. He wants to be top dog around here. You know, a big fish in a small pond. Max tends to cramp his style. It's family stuff." She laughed. "He's giving you a hard time because Max doesn't take enough notice of him."

"You mean, Joe knows I've been out with Max?"

Marina snorted. "Of course he knows. It's the

talk of the town, Libby. That's why the room was packed, this afternoon. Everyone wanted to get a look at you."

Libby's eyes threatened to pop out of her head. "You mean, they're judging me?" She glanced over her shoulder. The few stragglers left in the hall stood in small knots, staring at her, fascinated. Libby choked back fury, took a breath and stalked, fists clenched, eyes straight ahead, out through the door, as whispers chased close behind.

CHAPTER FOURTEEN

Mandy

The afternoon at Mangotsfield Hall had confirmed every one of Libby's fears about making a new life in a small town: gossip, cliques and the cold shoulder. London neighbours warned her, but she'd thought she knew best. So much for those great plans for opening a patisserie and chocolatier here. She was a laughing stock.

Safe at home, she grabbed a bottle of chardonnay from the fridge, filled a tall glass and took a satisfying gulp. As she drained the glass, and tilted the bottle again, ready for a top up, she caught sight of the clock. Mandy would be back soon, unless she'd changed her mind and found somewhere else to live, or returned home. Drinking wouldn't help. She'd better cook dinner, instead.

She screwed the top back on the wine bottle, replaced it in the fridge and rifled through, looking for food. She had plenty of vegetables and some chicken. A stir fry, maybe? Something sharp and satisfying, with lovely noodles to warm the stomach.

Libby chopped and tasted, blending soy sauce with chili. She crushed garlic, relishing the sharp scent and the bite on her tongue, her spirits rising.

The door crashed open. Mandy appeared, soaked to the skin, tattooed arms full of flowers. "These are for you." The girl blushed crimson, to the roots of the unnaturally black hair, plopped the flowers on the kitchen table, dropped a box of chocolates beside them, and walked out. "For being kind." Libby heard the glue of tears in Mandy's voice as she disappeared upstairs.

Libby wiped her own, suddenly damp eyes, ran cold water into a vase and cut the ends off the flower stems. She went to the foot of the stairs and shouted. "Thanks. I love Alstroemeria." She kept her voice matter-of-fact. "They last for ages."

Back in the kitchen, she turned on the radio, humming as she worked. A door closed upstairs and Mandy reappeared in dry clothes, wearing a sheepish grin. Libby longed to take a cloth to the girl's chalky face. Somewhere, under several inches of white make-up and lines of black kohl, hid a pretty face.

Libby reopened the wine, took out a clean glass and filled it, offering it to her new lodger. Mandy barely glanced at it, before taking a long swig. Libby winced. Now wasn't the moment to pontificate about wine-drinking, but it hurt to see good wine glugged like orange squash. Mandy said, "I heard about Joe Ramshore at the Hall."

"News really does travel fast, here, doesn't it?"

Mandy laughed. "You said it. Anyway, don't take any notice of him. He's a fool. By the way, I told Mum officially I've left home, and you know what? She said, 'Good for you.'"

"I'm sure she's glad. She worries about you. I know I—" Libby stopped. Mandy had enough problems without hearing a sob story about Libby's marriage. "Mothers worry about their children."

"Hmm. Maybe. Anyway, I told her to come over here if things get worse."

Libby swallowed. "Oh. Good idea."

"Don't worry, she won't come. At least, I don't think so…"

Every scrap of dinner eaten, they lounged around in the sitting room, eating chocolate and watching television. Libby fiddled with kindling and fire-lighters until a blaze started in the fire. She rested twigs and bigger shards of wood on top in an elaborate cone shape. "First fire of the year. Bet it goes out."

The smell of apple wood scented the room. Libby breathed in, tension leaving her shoulders as she curled her feet up on the sofa. Fuzzy lay across

Mandy's lap and purred loudly. "She never sits with me," Libby said. "She likes you."

Mandy dipped her head, cheeks reddening. "Mrs F, I've been meaning to ask you something."

"Ask away."

"You said you're going to open a patisserie."

Libby groaned. "That's the idea, or a chocolate shop. Sometimes it seems a very long way away. Don't tell Frank, he'll think I'm setting up in opposition to the bakery. I haven't decided yet. I've got a course coming up, about the business side." She wrinkled her nose. "Not my favourite thing. Still, I don't want to be bankrupt in my first week. Then, I need to get more experience, and I've got to finish writing this book. So, we're looking at months, if not years, before I get there."

"Well, when you do, I wondered—"

The phone rang. Libby, wishing she'd taken it off the hook, made a 'sorry' face at Mandy and answered. "It's me. In Los Angeles."

"Max. You're kidding. Really?"

"Really. I thought you'd want a progress report."

"Report away." She had things to say to Max when he got back, but they could wait.

He talked fast. "I saw Susie's husband, Mickey. He's a jerk."

"As we thought."

"Quite. Well, he said, and I quote, he was sorry Susie was dead, but he hadn't seen her for years and he's far too busy with a new family to come to the funeral. He doesn't know what Susie was doing here, and by the way, he wants to know if the will's been read yet. I suppose he's hoping to be in it."

"Is there a will?"

"Your guess is as good as mine. Susie never mentioned one."

"What about the rest of the band? Did you track them down?"

"Mickey's assistant gave me addresses." Libby heard a smile in his voice. "Nice girl." He'd have taken her out to dinner and pumped her for information. "Guy the violinist and James the keyboard player left years ago and went back to England. The addresses may be out of date, but it's a start. I asked her if she knew about Susie's solicitor, but she didn't. Said Susie left all the business to Mickey. I'm heading back."

"Back to Somerset? Not going to enjoy Los Angeles a while longer?"

He snorted. "Alone in a hotel? Not my idea of fun. How are things?"

She paused. She wouldn't tell him about Joe's verbal attack just now. Libby didn't want to get involved in family jealousies. "Fine."

"Good. What about Mrs Thomson?"

"She showed me photos."

The silence dragged on. "Photos?"

"Of Annie Rose. Didn't Mickey mention her?"

"Who's Annie Rose?"

He didn't know? "Mickey and Susie had a little girl who died when she was seven." The sharp intake of breath on the other end of the phone told Libby it was news to Max. "Susie sent cards, and photos of her daughter to Mrs Thomson. Mickey didn't think to mention her?"

"I'm speechless. Look, I'll be home late on Saturday. Let's meet on Sunday: lunch at the Lighthouse Inn."

"You'll be jet-lagged."

"I've got through it before. A glass of pinot noir does the trick."

Used to jet-setting around the world, then. Libby felt suddenly small and naïve. An afternoon in the local National Trust House, playing at dressing up, while Max flew half way around the world, probably club class. Bet he'd been everywhere. "Libby?"

"Yes?"

"Thought we'd been cut off."

"I was thinking. Can't you get back to Mickey and ask him about the little girl?"

"Tell you what. Email over a copy of the little

79

girl's photo for me to show him and I'll try."

Libby bit the inside of her cheek. She hadn't thought to ask for the photo, but she wasn't about to admit it. She'd have to nip back to Mrs Thomas's bungalow. She sighed. The car was in Jenkins' garage. "I'm in the middle of something, I'll send it this evening."

"OK. Mickey won't go to bed at 9 o'clock, I bet. He'll be out on the town with his trophy wife. The secretary will tell where he goes: I'm meeting her again at one of the bars here."

Of course you are. She couldn't resist you, could she? A nineteen-year-old.

"By the way. None of my business, but what exactly are you in the middle of?"

The cheek of the man. "Mandy's here. You know, from the bakery? She's come to-to…"

"To get away from her Dad?"

"Something like that."

"OK. Good idea. He's a menace. Send the photo as soon as you can, Libby. See you on Sunday."

Mandy appeared in the hall. Libby grabbed her keys. "I'm popping out for a minute."

"Can I come?"

Libby couldn't think of a reason to refuse. "We'll have to walk."

80

CHAPTER FIFTEEN

Breaking and Entering

"Mrs Thomson?" Libby rapped on the door. The light was on in the house, and she could hear the TV. Mrs Thomson must have turned the sound up. Libby banged again, harder, and pressed the bell, keeping her thumb on the buzzer, but no one came.

Mandy spoke from behind Libby's shoulder. "I'll go round the back." She disappeared. Libby kept up the banging and ringing, but no one came. Where was Bear? He should be barking his head off, by now.

Maybe Mrs Thomson had gone away. She might be visiting a friend, or a sister. "Libby. Get help." Mandy was back, panting. "I think she's had a fall."

Libby dialled 999, hand shaking. Not again. "Fire, police or ambulance?"

"Ambulance. Police. Both." Heart pounding, Libby followed Mandy to the back of the house, and peered through the kitchen window. The room gave nothing away: clean, neat and tidy as before; plates stacked on the draining board; tea towels folded over the sink to dry. Mandy grabbed Libby's arm and pointed. The door to the hall stood ajar, and through the gap, Libby caught a flash of green. She groaned. Mrs Thomson's slippers.

The door was locked. Libby shook it, but it held fast. She stood back, struggling to stay calm and sum up the problem. A pane of glass ran down the middle of the door. Libby gripped her phone in both hands and smashed it hard, into the panel. Broken shards clattered to the kitchen floor. She elbowed jagged fragments inwards, pulled the sleeve of her jacket down round her wrist, and slipped her arm through the door. The tips of her fingers touched the key. Grunting, she forced her shoulder further in, more splinters tinkling to the ground, until she could grab the key between thumb and finger and turn it in the lock.

Praying Mrs Thomson hadn't shot the bolt across as well, Libby leaned on the handle. The door swung open. She crunched across glass, and pushed open the inner door. The old lady lay at the foot of the stairs, the back of her head angled against the wall. Mandy whispered. "It looks as though her neck's broken."

Another body. A wave of nausea struck Libby. She swallowed it down. No time for that. She felt

82

Mrs Thomson's neck for a pulse, and fingered her wrist, horribly aware she'd done exactly the same for Susie. "I think she's dead."

Mandy's hand clamped to her mouth, muffling her voice. "She must have fallen down the stairs." She tugged Libby's elbow. "Can't we do anything? Shouldn't we put a blanket over her?"

"It's too late for that." A news programme still blared through the house. Libby's head pounded. She strode to the sitting room, found the remote control and switched off the TV. Silence fell. A cup of tea, half finished, sat in its saucer on the table. Mrs Thomson had been alone, with no one nearby to help when she fell. How long had she lain in the hall?

The house was quiet: too quiet. What was wrong? *Bear.* Where was the dog? Why hadn't he barked when his mistress fell? A cold hand tugged at Libby's chest. She stepped with care around Mrs Thomson and set off up the stairs. "Where are you going?" Mandy squeaked.

"The dog's missing." Libby went through the house, opening one door after another. "Bear, where are you? Come on out, it's me."

Mandy sat on the stairs, transfixed by Mrs Thomson's body. "Maybe he's outside?"

Before Libby could search the garden, horns blared, lights flashed and the emergency services

83

arrived in force. Joe Ramshore was first. "Mrs Forest. What are you doing here?"

Mandy said. "We found Mrs Thomson."

"Did you?" He frowned at Libby, eyes narrowed, suspicious. The ambulance crew whispered in his ear. "Another body," he said. "And once again, you're on the spot." He took Libby's arm. "Might I ask what you were doing here?"

***

The wooden chair at the police station, designed for utility rather than comfort, made Libby's back ache. She stared ahead at uninviting walls, bare of pictures, or notices, painted dull grey. Mandy sat next to her at the plain wooden table, swirling cold, undrinkable tea inside a paper cup. Detective Sergeant Ramshore tilted his chair back, until only two legs touched the floor, waiting blank-faced for an explanation. "We went to the house to look at a photo. Mrs Thomson showed it to me earlier when I walked the dog for her."

His expression didn't change. "You were looking after Bear?"

"Max—your father—he's away."

Joe's eyes were cold. He raised one eyebrow in disbelief. "And he asked you to take over the dog walking?"

Libby held his glance. "Why not?"

84

He shrugged. "So, you came back here in the evening, to visit an old woman? Didn't you realise you'd frighten her at this time of night? It looks like she tried to get to the door, wearing her ragged old slippers, and tripped on the stairs."

"What?" Furious, Libby leaned forward. "Are you saying it's my fault?"

"Have you got a better idea?"

"The dog's missing. Maybe she was going out to look for him?"

Joe crossed an ankle over the other leg, tapping his cup with a long finger. "We'd know more about that if you hadn't broken in, making such a mess of the back door, wouldn't we?"

"We had to get in." Libby was indignant. "What if she'd still been alive?"

"OK." He uncrossed his legs. "Fair enough, I suppose. Anyway, I'm afraid the poor old soul's gone. She must have been almost ninety, and she lived all on her own. Something like this was bound to happen, one day."

"You think it's an accident, then?"

The detective laughed. "Mrs Forest, please don't start imagining someone murdered Mrs Thomson. Old ladies fall all the time. It's amazing she lasted so long, all alone in this place. No one broke in. The only damage is to the kitchen door, thanks to you."

85

"Can we go home, then?"

When Joe smiled, he looked like his father. "I'll get one of my men to drive you." Tired, Libby and Mandy trudged along the drab corridor of the police station. "And Mrs Forest."

She stopped. "Yes?"

"Try not to find any more bodies for a few days."

CHAPTER SIXTEEN

Bear's Adventure

Libby tapped out a brief text for Max before she fell, exhausted, into bed. *Can't send photo after all. Explain later. Please text addresses of band members.* She was asleep even before the whooshing noise warned the text had gone.

A series of messages greeted Libby when she woke. *What's going on? Hope everything OK. Here are addresses.* Libby smiled. Max was no more able to use text speak, full of gr8 and thx, than she. She copied the addresses onto a scrap of paper and folded it, sliding it into a pocket in her handbag.

"I'm worried about Bear." She poured cornflakes into a bowl. Mandy, white faced, a faded grey dressing gown pulled up to her chin, looked like a vampire. She cradled a coffee cup in both hands, and grunted. Libby hid a smile. It was good to have a teenager about the place again, failing to communicate. "I'm going back to see what happened."

"You know it's not half past six yet, don't you?"

Libby chopped a banana into tiny pieces and

dropped them into her bowl. "I can't just leave him." Anyway, she wanted to get to the house early. There was a job she must do alone.

Mandy heaved a sigh and pushed herself up from the table. "I'll come with you."

"No. I got you into enough trouble yesterday. If Detective Sergeant Ramshore finds out we've been back, we'll go straight to the top of the suspect list. That is, when he works out Mrs Thomson didn't fall."

Mandy's mouth hung open. "You think she was pushed?"

"Of course, she was. How many unexplained sudden deaths does a place like Exham have in the average week? Yet, here are two in a few days."

"There are lots of old people, here. You know, in Haven House and that new place near the kid's playground. There must be dozens of people dying every week."

"Susie wasn't old. Anyway, it's too much of a coincidence." Libby stirred the banana into her cereal. "Think about it. She comes back to Exham for some reason, we don't know why. Next minute, she's dead. Then, one of the few people who really cared about her dies." She pointed her spoon at Mandy. "I was beginning to think the police were right, and Susie's death was suicide, but this is one coincidence too many."

Mandy got to her feet and stacked her bowl in the dishwasher. "In that case, I'll come with you. You can't go alone. Someone has to keep you out of trouble."

Libby choked on her cornflakes. "Nonsense. I'll be careful. Anyway, one of us needs to get over to the shop. Frank can't bake bread and serve at the same time."

Libby enjoyed the walk to Mrs Thomson's house. The wind had died away overnight, and the rain dried. She'd take Shipley out soon. She'd been neglecting him a bit, deserting the poor animal for Bear. They'd have a good run on the beach, maybe later, before the weather broke again. A pale sun peeped out once or twice from between heavy clouds that threatened more storms before long.

As expected, the police had boarded up Mrs Thomson's back door. Libby walked on, out into the half-acre garden. The late Mr Thomson's retirement pride and joy looked neglected, the pond full of duckweed and dead leaves. A few remnants of foliage clung to grey overhanging branches. Beds of roses had run to a riot of hips and haws. Something for the birds to enjoy, at least.

Libby called, softly. "Bear?" No answer. She called again, and whistled. What was that? She strained her ears. The sound had come from her right, where a sturdy shed nestled against a ragged yew hedge. Libby tugged at the door until it creaked open. Bear sprawled in the corner. He raised his massive head, staggered to his feet, whined, wobbled and lay down again.

Libby's stomach heaved as she caught the acrid scent of sick. A pool of vomit stank nearby. Fresh scratches covered the shed door, where the dog had tried to get out. Bear whined again, and lay, head on paws, exhausted. "What happened to you, Bear?"

The shed was clean and warm, and a selection of doggy toys suggested Bear sometimes slept there. His basket was lined with old sweaters, positioned close to an empty bowl. Judging by the nearby splashes, it had recently held water. Another container held a lump of meat, half-eaten. Bear had only taken a bite or two.

Libby rubbed her knuckles against the top of his bony head. The dog nuzzled her hand. "What did they give you? You're on the mend, old thing, but I'll take you to the vet to make sure." She straightened up. "But first, I need to get into the house." There was a tool box in the shed. Libby grinned. This was going to be easier than she'd thought.

The lock on the back door was still broken. The police had nailed hardboard roughly across the opening, half to the door, the rest attached to the side posts. She'd better be quick. A locksmith would be arriving this morning.

She opened the tool box, glanced round to check she was alone, grasped the biggest hammer firmly, hooked the claw behind the first nail and twisted. The nail popped out. So did the second. The third was awkward, bending and sticking, and Libby's hair stuck to her head with sweat by the time she wrenched it out.

As she levered out the fourth and final nail, the door swung open and she stepped inside. The broken glass had been swept away. She tiptoed into the front room, stopped and straightened. No need to tread with such care; there was no one in the house to hear her. She let her gaze rove across the crowded tables and shelves. Nothing had changed since she'd been here with Mrs Thomson.

The old lady's presence seemed all around. Libby shivered and whispered, "I hope they didn't scare you, before they shoved you down the stairs." Maybe they took her by surprise, and she had no idea what happened. Or perhaps it was someone Mrs Thomson knew and trusted. Lonely, she would have let them in, just as she'd welcomed Libby. "I won't mess up your house, I promise. I just need those photographs."

The album lay where she'd last seen it, among a

pile of notebooks and scraps of paper. "I'll find out who killed Suzanne," Libby promised. She started to flick through the stack of papers, fingers fumbling. Her head flew up. What was that noise? Someone was outside.

She grabbed the pile of papers and books, along with the album, and thrust them all into her shoulder bag. Just in time. The door flew open. "What the—" Detective Sergeant Ramshore slid to a halt, halfway between Libby and the door, arms folded. "Mrs Forest. I might have known. This is breaking and entering, you know."

Libby thought fast. "I'm worried about the dog. I came back to find him."

Joe hooked his thumbs into his belt. "Well, one of my men found him in the shed. Looks like he slept there last night, so you can go home again, Mrs Forest, and please, please, just stay away."

"I was going to take him home with me."

Joe's face cleared. "Good idea. Make yourself useful. And don't come back." He stood aside and Libby slipped past, shoulder bag heavy. Sometimes, age and gender had its uses. He'd have spent longer talking to a pretty young girl, and he'd have been suspicious of a man, but a woman of a certain age, old enough to be his mother... Maybe he'd decided Libby was just a foolish, interfering older woman. She bit her lip to keep a tell-tale smile from her face.

"Wait." Joe held up a hand. Libby stopped, heart racing. She'd celebrated too soon. Was he about to search the bag? She'd have a job explaining the stack of stolen papers. "I've got some news. I suppose you're entitled to hear it first, as you found her."

"About Mrs Thomson?" Libby stood sideways, her bag clasped under the arm furthest away from the officer, her body shielding it from view.

"No, about Susie Bennett. The post mortem shows more bruising than we thought: more than the pathologist thinks would result from being thrown about in a storm."

"Bruising? What does that mean?" No harm in continuing to play the innocent woman.

"It means you may be right, crazy as it sounds. Susie Bennett might, just possibly, have been murdered."

"Do you—do you know who did it?"

He leaned back, legs set apart, every inch the bold investigator. "Not yet. I'll be surprised if we ever find out. A body on the beach, in the storm. No evidence, you see. Still, don't leave town, Mrs Forest." Libby slipped out of the room, clutching the bag tight to her body.

Joe had already lost interest in her. "Better get the door fixed right now, Evans, before the rest of

93

the town comes to visit."

By the time she arrived home, Bear trooping, listless, beside her, Libby's shoulder ached from the weight of books. Her mind raced. As she'd turned to leave Mrs Thomson's sitting room, she'd glanced out of the window. From there, the widow could see right along the beach, to the pier on the left and the lighthouse to the right.

What if Mrs Thomson had stood, looking out into the storm, on Monday night? She might have seen something unusual. More than the storm and high tide. Something that had got her killed.

CHAPTER SEVENTEEN

Guy

The faithful old Citroen was due for collection today. Libby checked the time. Yes, she could pick up the car and visit both band members today, as Mandy had volunteered to take over Shipley's walk.

Bear recovered fast, growing perkier every moment until he bounded up and down the hall with his usual vigour. How long could Libby keep a dog his size in this tiny cottage?

Oh, well, she'd worry about that later. Meanwhile, she dug out an ancient apple crate from the cupboard under the stairs, dragged it into a warm spot in the hall and lined it with old blankets. "There you are, my lad." She took a step into the kitchen and held her breath. Fuzzy lay curled by the door, in a spot where underground water pipes heated the floor. Bear loomed over her, panting.

Was Libby about to witness an epic fight? Fuzzy stood and stretched. What was that noise? No. Surely not. Libby laughed. The cat was purring. "When did you two make friends?" The animals ignored her. Bear leaned over, touched his nose to Fuzzy, and settled down next to his new buddy.

Libby stashed Mrs Thomson's photo album in a drawer and walked to the garage. She'd spend the evening poring through the book for clues.

Alan Jenkins wiped oily hands on a blue overall. "Ah. Mrs Forest, there you are. She's just about ready for you." Why did men always call cars, 'she'?

He still insisted on refusing payment. "Tell Max it's a present." He'd even topped the Citroen up with petrol. Was Max some kind of Godfather, around here?

Tired of arguing, Libby held out a packet of shortbread. Alan's eyes lit up. "You're a good woman." What was it they said about the way to a man's heart being through his stomach?

***

The road to Bath twisted through tiny villages, along a road too narrow for more than one car. Marina told her it was quicker by train, but Libby needed the car. She'd made up her mind to visit both the other members of Susie's old, defunct band, before Max returned. James the keyboard player lived just outside Bristol, and Guy the violinist lived in Bath.

She'd thrown a ham salad into a Tupperware container before setting off, and she pulled over, by the side of the Chew Valley Lake, to eat. She took a bite and screwed up her nose. The dressing didn't taste quite right. Maybe a little too much lemon juice? Or not enough honey? She'd make up another batch soon.

It was days since she'd had time to potter around in the kitchen, experimenting. Once this business was over, she planned to lock herself in for hours and get on with the book. The publisher's deadline was looming. Libby felt a twinge inside at the thought. She planned a series of excuses as she ate, opening the door to let a few rays of sunshine warm her. *Dead husband: that would do it.* At least it had the advantage of being true.

She threw a crust of bread into the water. Excited ducks scrambled over one another. Libby took out a chunk of sultana cake. The ducks wouldn't get any of this, her favourite comfort food.

Every last crumb eaten, she climbed back into the car, crunching gears in sudden excitement. Maybe Guy would have some answers.

His double-fronted Georgian house stood, white-painted, in a block of similar graceful homes. He flung the door open almost before she'd had time to drop the brass lion-head knocker, as if he'd been expecting her.

The man's appearance took her aback. She'd been prepared for aging hippy long hair, flares or tasselled waistcoat. Instead, his short, neat haircut, shirt, and the final touch, a silk tie with a Windsor knot, were conventional enough to please Libby's parents. He was only a short step away from a cardigan.

His lined face wore the slightly anxious look of a middle-aged man, whose mirror proves his youth is disappearing fast. He led her inside. "Max rang to say you'd be coming." So it was Max who gave the game away. Annoying man. She'd lost the element of surprise. "Anyway," Guy shrugged. "Susie was all over the local news. I thought I'd hear something from Exham. When's the funeral?

Was the man upset? Libby couldn't tell. The pupils of his eyes were big and dark. He pushed wire-rimmed glasses further up a long nose, and waved at a selection of wines and spirits on a breakfast bar. "Drink?"

The huge, airy kitchen was clean and, unlike Guy himself, at the cutting edge of modern design. Libby flicked her gaze round the room, finding no sign of a wife or children among the uncompromising shine of black granite and glassy smooth white paint. She shook her head. "I'm driving, but I'd love a coffee."

"Ah. Good choice." A wannabe barista? Guy clattered around the huge, gleaming chrome of the coffee machine with milk jugs and coffee. Libby hid a smile. Whatever had happened to Kenco and hot water?

The coffee, when it arrived at last, was perfect. "So, you found Susie on the beach. That's sad. Not quite the dramatic end I'd expect of her. She'd have preferred something outrageous, like a mistimed bungee jump." When he smiled, he showed beautiful white teeth. They must be the result of the band's success in America. "The drink, was it?"

There was no reason to hide the truth. "In fact, she had been drinking, but it looks more like murder."

That caught the man's attention. He blinked. "Seriously?"

Libby pressed on, glad to have dented his calm surface. Now, maybe he'd forget any prepared speeches. "There are a few suspects. I imagine the police will visit you, soon."

A flash of consciousness, a widening of the eyes, told Libby she'd hit a nerve. He glanced around the kitchen, and she realised what had seemed odd about him. His gaze vague, eyes dark, behaviour too casual. The man was stoned. Libby wondered where he kept the drugs. "Excuse me." He stepped outside the kitchen, into the hall, and called up the stairs. "Alvin?"

"Yeah. What is it?" A younger man, in his twenties, hair longer, mussed up, sleeveless t-shirt showing muscled arms, leaned over the banisters.

"Clean things up, will you?"

The younger man frowned, puzzled for a moment, then his brow cleared. "Right. OK."

Libby gulped down the coffee. She had to get her questions out before he cut their conversation short. He'd want time to clear the house of incriminating drug paraphernalia. "I just wanted to find out about Susie. What happened after all those albums, when she came back to Exham, and why? Those sorts of things."

He shrugged. "Don't ask me. Didn't know she was here. The band broke up, years ago, and we all lost touch. We made a bit of money. I had enough to buy this place." He looked around the kitchen, beaming. "Bought a house for my mother, as well. She's in a care home, now, but she had a good few years."

"What about Susie's marriage?"

The smile faded. He shrugged. "Usual showbiz thing. Mickey found a newer, younger model. You know: longer legs, blonder hair. Anyway, Susie lost her spark when..."

He stopped, licked his lips and shot a sideways glance at Libby. She let the pause go on as she rinsed her cup and dried it, but Guy showed no sign of telling her any more details. She'd have to prompt. "OK. I know about the little girl that died. Annie."

"Annie Rose, yeah. Cute little thing." The lines on Guy's face softened. Libby glimpsed a warmer, kinder man somewhere under the surface. "Broke Susie's heart when little Annie died."

"And Mickey's too?"

"What? Oh, yeah, of course. He was upset. We all were. That's when Susie said she couldn't go on. We tried to talk her out of it, but who could blame her? Something like that, cuts you right up. She left LA, went up north, heading for Canada. She had some sort of connections there; distant family, or something. She was a bit vague."

"Has she been in touch?"

"Nope. Clean break. I came back to Bath, took an OU course in computing."

Libby laughed aloud. "Computing? After life in a band?"

He pushed his glasses up again. "Well, I'd always done the techie stuff. I played violin a bit, sure, but I'd rather tinker with the sound system." He shrugged again. "Not really cut out for travelling. It was good to get off the road and

101

settle down."

"Apart from the drugs."

He shuffled his feet. "Just weed and occasional coke at weekends. Nothing heavy."

"Anything else you can tell me about Susie?"

"She was a nice kid. If I'd known she was in England I'd have got in touch."

Alvin shambled into the kitchen, scratching at an unshaven chin, and Libby beat a retreat. Guy seemed to know as little about Susie as her old school mates in Exham. It was as though she'd been a ghost, passing through people's lives.

One question above all others hammered in Libby's head. What on earth had Susie been doing in Exham after all those years away?

CHAPTER EIGHTEEN

James

Libby fiddled with the satnav, planning the route to Weldon, on the outskirts of Bristol, well aware that someone, either Guy or Alvin, watched from a window. They wanted to make sure she'd left the area. She revved the engine and wound down the window, waving with enthusiasm. That would give them something to think about.

The route to James Sutcliffe's home took Libby down a series of ever more winding, narrow roads. She stopped to check her iPhone. Surely no one lived down this tiny, overgrown lane, hedges high on either side?

No signal. Should she give up, reverse back and go home? A horn blared and Libby twisted in her seat. She flinched. A monster tractor filled the whole of the rear window. The engine ground to a halt at the last moment, inches away.

The driver dragged off a pair of headphones, swung down from the cab, and rolled across to her window. A knitted jumper of indeterminate colour lay, unravelling, over his paunch. His head, stubbly and weathered, barely reached above the window. He shoved a ruddy, belligerent face close to the glass. "Where you off to, then?

He'd left Libby no space to open the Citroen's door. Trapped and furious, she lowered the window, and used her iciest voice. "What business is it of yours?"

"If you're on the way to Ross, you need to go back and turn right onto the main road. And don't use the Satnav."

"How can I go back with your tractor practically in my back seat? Anyway," she remembered why she was here. "I'm looking for James Sutcliffe. I think he lives nearby."

"Ah." The eyes narrowed. "Huh. Plenty like you come up here, on the way to Ross. No more sense than the day they're born. Buy an expensive Satnav, throw away perfectly good maps and get lost here, in my lane. You're going nowhere this way, let me tell you."

Libby picked out information from an apparently well-practised rant. "Your lane? You must be Mr Sutcliffe."

"So, who wants me?" Must they have the conversation here? Libby peered ahead, but she couldn't see round the corner.

The cultured voice of the satnav recovered and broke in, insisting that in one hundred yards she would reach her destination. Libby pulled out the connection. "I want to ask about Susie Bennett."

"Thought so." James Sutcliffe was triumphant. The colour in his cheeks, previously the sort of dull pink a kind observer would describe as a healthy, open air glow, darkened to purple. Was he about to have a stroke? At least that would stop him blowing Libby's head off with a shotgun. "Just get off my land, woman. I've had enough of journalists, nosing into my business."

"No, no, I'm not a journalist." The squeak in Libby's voice was less than convincing.

"Who says so?" The man had a good point. It was one thing to prove you were something: journalists carried ID cards, didn't they, like police officers? Much harder to prove you were nothing of the sort, just a normal person. Not that Libby felt very normal, given the events of the past few days.

She slapped on what she hoped was a non-journalistic smile, aiming for a mix of seriousness and reason. "Anyway, even if I was from a newspaper, I can't go back until you move your tractor."

Sutcliffe growled. "Get yourself up to the yard." He stomped back to the tractor.

The vast front end was only inches from her car. Libby feared for the newly repaired Citroen.

105

She clashed gears and cursed under her breath. The car lurched further up the lane, finally rounding the corner to rest on a cobbled farmyard.

Mud, an inch thick, covered uneven cobbles. Libby groaned. She'd chosen her shoes with care: elegant red patent with kitten heels and elaborate holes cut into the sides. Wholly appropriate for the refined ambience of Georgian Bath, they were unlikely to survive an encounter with farmyard muck. The temptation to wheel round and disappear back up the lane was almost overwhelming.

Holding the door for support, feet slithering, she edged out of the car. "Mr Sutcliffe, I'm honestly not from the media. I've just been talking to Guy. Guy Miles." The farmer frowned, recognising the name. Libby held out her phone. "Ring him, if you like."

Libby had never heard anyone harrumph before, but that was what Sutcliffe did. He brushed past the outstretched phone. "Better come in, then."

She ducked under a low doorway that opened into a huge kitchen. Mud from the yard had infiltrated, using the convenient transport of Sutcliffe's boots, through the ill-fitting door. It carpeted the otherwise bare, flagstone floor of a rustic room, apparently undecorated since the

1950s. Rickety orange boxes, stacked underneath and to the side of a huge, pine table, teetered and trembled. Libby caught a glimpse of greaseproof paper and a logo, showing a goat's head. Sutcliffe, proving himself to be no more of a talker indoors than in the lane, uttered one word. "Cheese."

CHAPTER NINETEEN

Cheese

"Dairy's over there." He pointed through the window. To be sure, behind the run-down farmhouse nestled a contrasting complex of neat brick buildings, doors and windows smart with red paint, enclosing a small yard lined with pristine paving stones. In the distance, a herd of goats tugged up mouthfuls of grass in a paddock, as though on a mission. "Jack runs the business, now."

The unexpected burst of information brought Libby back to the filthy kitchen. Could that be pride, in the farmer's voice? "Jack?" She guessed. "Your son?"

"Ah. Lives over yonder with that fancy wife of his." Sutcliffe's ruddy face had calmed. Social relations had somehow been restored. The farmer gestured towards a battered brown kettle. "Tea?"

"Yes, please. Let me get the cups." Many more of these visits and she'd float away on a tide of tea and coffee. She pulled mugs from the wobbling pile on the draining board and seized the opportunity to inspect them for grime. She'd seen worse.

Sutcliffe fiddled with kettle and tea caddy. Libby coughed. "Susie Bennett. You were in the band, with her and Guy, isn't that right?"

"Ah." Sutcliffe kept his back turned.

"I found her body."

He stopped, kettle poised, inches above an ancient, cracked teapot. His words were almost inaudible. "Did you now? All alone on the beach?"

The bluster drained away from the red face, leaving it crumpled, like a crushed eggshell. Libby took the kettle, pouring hot water into the pot, giving the farmer time to blow a loud nasal blast on a grubby handkerchief. "Little Susie. Who'd have thought it?"

The door opened and a younger, taller, cleaner version of James Sutcliffe strode in. Any hope the son would prove more welcoming than his father evaporated. He threw a cursory glance at Libby. "What's going on, here, Dad?"

Sutcliffe wiped his eyes. Libby assessed the distance to the door, wishing she could just leave, annoyed to have misread James Sutcliffe. The gruff exterior hid deep feelings. "I–I'm sorry." Lost for adequate words, she sniffed a nearby bottle of milk, decided there was life left in it, and poured three cups of tea. "I came to find out more about Susie Bennett."

"You've picked a bad time." The son pulled out a wooden chair and his father sank into it. "Dad's wife died a month ago. The news about Susie just about finished him off."

Libby gulped. No wonder the place was such a mess. James Sutcliffe had been running on empty, trying to keep going after the tragedy. Jack Sutcliffe had said, "Dad's wife." She wasn't his own mother, then.

He folded his arms. "What's it all to do with you, anyway?"

"I found her body. On the beach, under the lighthouse. I just wanted to find out more about her. The police aren't interested, but she'd been away for so long…"

"The lighthouse?" James Sutcliffe interrupted. "That's where we used to do our courting, back along when we were lads. Bonfires on the beach, hanky-panky in the dunes." Libby studied the rugged face, searching for a likeness to the youth in the photograph. Life had been hard for Susie's old friend.

Jack opened a series of jars. He held one out. "Rich tea?"

Libby dunked one in her cup. "I just wanted to find out if anyone knew why Susie was back in England."

The older Sutcliffe stuffed his handkerchief in a pocket, packed a biscuit into his mouth and mumbled. "Came to see my Mary."

His son translated. "Susie wanted to see my stepmother, before she died. It was cancer. Took a long time for her to go."

It was as simple as that: no mystery, after all. Susie had come back to visit old friends in trouble. "I'm very sorry for your loss."

Sutcliffe's son filled in the details. James married his first wife in the United States before the band broke up. The marriage didn't last long: the first Mrs Sutcliffe had a sharp eye for business. She left her husband and young son for an aging but rich American tycoon. Susie stayed in touch when the newly divorced James brought his son, Jack, home to the UK and turned to farming.

"She used to write, now and then." Jack smiled. "Even sent me presents from America. T-shirts and sneakers: things you couldn't get in England, then. Like an aunt, really."

"Do you have any letters?"

Sutcliffe shrugged. "Threw them away. Anyway, they were private." Libby held up a hand. "I'm not being nosy, Mr Sutcliffe. You see, no one knows exactly what happened. How Susie died, I mean. It seemed like she'd been drinking or taking drugs, and got caught in the high tide."

Sutcliffe snorted. "Susie wouldn't get caught. She grew up in Exham. Knew every inch of the beach. She'd never let the tide catch her, like one of those summer visitors. She drank like a fish, mind you, that's true enough."

Libby smiled. "You must have known her daughter?" She looked from one man to the other. "I heard Annie Rose drowned."

Sutcliffe clenched his fists and hammered them on the table, rattling the mugs. "If I could get my hands on that man…" He pointed a finger at Libby. "Neglect. That's what killed Susie's little girl. Mickey Garston let her die because he was too lazy to look after her."

"Dad." Jack intervened, one hand on his father's arm. "No one really knows what happened. Anyway, that was years ago. It's Susie's death we're talking about." He looked at Libby. "You're saying it might have been suicide?"

Libby shrugged. "Or murder." She let that thought sink in.

Sutcliffe clattered the mugs together and threw them in the sink. "Mickey Garston. That's who's behind it, you mark my words. Susie cursed the day she met that man. Just let me get at him…" Jack laid a hand on his father's shoulder, but the older man shrugged it off. "Should have dealt with him myself, years ago."

"Mickey was in America when she died," Libby said. "Besides, why would he want her dead after so many years?"

"I'll show you." Sutcliffe left the room. Libby heard drawers opening, papers being shuffled. "Here it is." He held out two pages of writing paper. He hadn't thrown all her letters away, then.

Libby glanced at the signature. *Love, Susie, xxx.* She read through the childish script.

Dear Jamie and Mary,

Thank you for the beautiful flowers you sent, and for remembering the anniversary of Annie Rose's death. She would have been ten years old. I still can't believe she's gone.

I miss England very much, but I won't come back. I have friends out here and the sun always shines. Most important, though, is I can visit Annie Rose's grave to talk to her.

You probably heard Mickey and I split up. It's been all over the news programmes. He wants me to divorce him, but I'll never do it. Why should I set him free, after all he's done? My mistake was marrying him in the first place.

I want him to be miserable..."

Libby re-read the letter. "No divorce?" She let the idea take root in her brain. "That means Mickey isn't her ex-husband. I suppose he's her widower, now. But that can't be right, surely. Everyone knows Mickey's married to Jenna Fielding."

113

Sutcliffe rocked his chair back. "Susie wouldn't give Mickey a divorce."

Libby was still thinking it through. "I don't blame her. If she'd made enough money, she wouldn't need to rely on Mickey for alimony, and divorces get messy. Anyway, who cares if Mickey and Jenna aren't married? What difference does it make?"

Sutcliffe laughed, the sound sharp as a whip crack. "It matters when there's money at stake." He shook his head. "You have to understand Susie, you see. Most people don't. At school, she was a bit of an outcast, because her parents were travellers. Her mother came from an old gypsy family. As for her dad, he was long gone when she was just a bairn."

"Susie's parents never bothered to get married. No one knows what happened to her old man: he'll have died, long ago. Travellers live free as air, but they don't live long. Her Ma died while we were in the states. Anyway, our Susie wouldn't give that man a divorce."

"She was more of a gypsy than anyone I've ever met. She didn't care about money. She did things the traveller's way: with a handshake. I'd be willing to bet my farm, she died without leaving a will. Probably didn't even have a solicitor."

"That means Susie's money…"

Sutcliffe slapped the table with one hand. "It means, as they were still married, Mickey inherits the whole of Susie's fortune."

CHAPTER TWENTY

Mushroom Sauce

Libby's bones ached as she turned into the town. It was getting dark. She longed to get home to her cottage, close the curtains to shut out the world, light the sitting room with the gentle glow of table lamps, collapse onto into the comfortable sofa and think.

If only Max were here, she could run today's discoveries past him. Had he found out any more about Mickey? Susie's husband had an alibi, but that didn't mean he couldn't mastermind Susie's death from the other side of the Atlantic.

She yawned and drove onto the drive. She'd hardly had time to think about Mrs Thomson's fall. Had the old lady been pushed: killed for something she'd seen through the wind and rain of Monday night? Libby shivered. Two women were dead and the local police weren't bothering to investigate. She felt very alone. If she didn't persist, Susie and Mrs Thomson would be forgotten.

Later, she'd look through the photos in the old

lady's album. Who knew what else she might uncover from Susie's past? But first, she needed a large glass of wine. Her mouth watered in anticipation as she parked the car in the drive, fumbled in her bag for keys, and unlocked the door.

As it opened, a wave of noise erupted. Mandy, the Goth. Libby had forgotten all about her. Televisions blared from every downstairs room. Above the racket, Mandy was singing, tuneless but enthusiastic. Libby shouted. "Mandy." She waited. "Mandy." She clattered up the stairs to hammer on the door of Mandy's room.

The door swung open. "Oh, hello, Libby." Mandy, eyes wide, covered her mouth with one hand and pulled an earphone off one ear. "Sorry, am I too noisy? Mum thumps on the ceiling with a broom handle when she wants me to shut up."

Libby's exasperation dissolved. Having Mandy around reminded her of the recent, bitter-sweet days, when her own noisy teenagers lived with her, shoes and bags littering the hallway, damp towels everywhere and the fridge emptied as fast as she filled it. The angry retort died on her lips. "Is chicken and chips OK for dinner?"

"Wow, wonderful. With some of that special sauce you told me about?"

"Ready in half an hour."

Libby opened a bottle of pinot noir. If Mandy was going to stay, it was time to wean her off sweet white fizz. Forgetting the tired ache in her back, Libby set about preparations with enthusiasm. She made salad dressing, sliced potatoes into chips, washed vegetables and fried a handful of chestnut mushrooms in olive oil. In a minute or too, she'd add some crushed garlic, a slug of brandy, a whisk of mustard and a dollop of cream, and the sauce would be perfect.

She breathed in garlic and olive oil, the scent of sunshine and happiness. Mandy burst into the kitchen. "Mm. Smells good."

Libby handed over a glass, one third full. "Sit down, Mandy. You're not to take a single mouthful yet."

"What? Why not?"

"You'll enjoy it more, this way. Trust me." Mandy rolled her eyes, but waited, glass in hand. "Now, just circle the glass in your hand, so the air gets at the wine. That's it. Be gentle," as Mandy's wine threatened to spill over the top of the glass. "Now, have a look at the colour. Gorgeous, isn't it? OK, now get your nose in the glass and sniff."

Mandy giggled and put on a fake, affected wine-tasting voice. "I'm getting peaches, brambles and a spot of manure." Libby threw a tea towel at her. "Maybe I need another glass to be sure."

"Wait a minute, here's the food."

Libby served the chicken breasts. Mandy spooned salad from the oversized wooden bowl onto her plate. "Mmm. Scrumptious."

"Had a good day at the shop?"

"Your new recipe went down well. What about your day? Made any discoveries?"

"Not about Mrs Thomson, I'm afraid, but I found one or two things about Susie."

Mandy's phone rang. She bit her lip. "It's Mum." She pressed the button and her voice rose. "Calm down, Mum, I can't hear you."

The voice on the other end of the phone sounded scared. Mandy's hand shook as she covered the phone. She hissed at Libby. "It's Dad. He's having one of his tempers—stomping around upstairs and shouting."

"Tell your Mum to come over here. She mustn't stay there. No, wait, I'll go and get her."

Mandy relayed the message to her hysterical mother. "No, Mum, stay there, but keep an eye out. Libby's coming." Her voice rose. "Mum, I can hear him. Get out of the house!"

Libby ran to the car and accelerated away, tyres screaming. The drive took less than three minutes. She screeched to a halt, just as Mandy's mother, coatless despite the cold, ran out, fumbling at the car door. Libby leaned over to release the catch and Elaine half-fell into the car, shivering, cheeks wet with tears, teeth chattering so she could barely speak. "I s-sneaked out the back door when Bert went to get b-beer from the fridge."

Bert burst through the front door, bottle raised, and Elaine screamed. Libby stepped on the accelerator. "It's OK." The Citroen roared away from the curb, heading for home. "Just in time."

Home in minutes, Libby slotted the safety chain firmly in place on the front door while Mandy took her mother's arm and settled her in the kitchen, still trembling. "Did he hit you?" A cut on Elaine's forehead oozed blood.

She flinched. "No. I—I banged it—"

"Ran into a door, did you? I don't think so." Libby dipped cotton wool in warm water laced with Dettol, and dabbed at the cut. "It's not deep. I shouldn't think you need stitches, but you do have to ring the police."

Elaine pushed Libby's hand away. "No. Bert's had too much to drink, that's all it is. It'll be fine when he sobers up."

"Mum." Tears started in Mandy's eyes. "It won't be fine. He'll get drunk tomorrow and do it again, you know he will. Please ring the police."

Elaine shook her head. "I know what's best, Mandy. Just let him be. He'll cool off."

A heavy blow shook the front door. Libby

120

leaped to her feet. "If Bert's cooled off, then who's that?" Another crash echoed round the house, then a third. A male voice bellowed, but Libby couldn't make out the words. The three women were on their feet, searching for something—anything—they could use to defend themselves.

Mandy grabbed Libby's arm. "He's come after us. What are we going to do?"

"We're going to tell him to go home." Libby's stomach lurched. Bert was well-built and strong. The bad back that kept him on sick pay was pure fiction. He could stop hammering on her door, though. How dare he? "Stay here, you two."

Libby straightened her shoulders, strode to the front door and pulled it open a few inches, the chain keeping it safe. Bert thrust his head into the gap. Libby could make out every mark on the man's red face: black, open pores on a bulbous nose, blobs of sweat above a mean top lip and deep lines on an angry brow. Spit flew from the thin mouth. "You little…"

"Don't you dare speak to me like that, Mr Parsons. There are three of us here, and we're phoning the police at this very moment."

Mandy had followed, close behind, phone to one ear. "Yeah, Dad. Go home and sober up." Bert Parsons swore and kicked the door. The chain rattled. Libby took a pace back, bile in her throat. She was vaguely aware of clattering from the kitchen, as Bert kicked again. Helpless, Libby watched as the screws holding the chain on the door sprang out, clinking as they hit the floor.

CHAPTER TWENTY-ONE

Chicken and Chips

The third kick burst the door open. Bert lurched inside and shoved Libby in the chest. "Get out here, wife," he roared.

A growl echoed down the hall. Mouth open, teeth bared, Bear leapt at the intruder. Bert stumbled back. The dog growled again, and reared, enormous paws on Bert's shoulders. Bert tried to turn, slipped, and fell. Bear dropped to all fours, panting and slavering above him.

Saliva dripped on Bert's face. He struggled to get up, one arm ready to fend off the dog. "Get that animal away from me." Bear planted both forepaws firmly on Bert's chest and howled. The noise was deafening.

"Well done, Bear." Suddenly, Max was in the hallway, hands on hips. He grinned at Libby, whose stomach performed a leap of relief. "But, it looks as though I've arrived too late for the excitement."

Libby, heart still pounding, hauled the dog off Bert, and scratched Bear's ears. "Good dog." She slipped her fingers through the dog's collar. "Mandy, why don't you take Bear into the kitchen and find a treat for him?"

Elaine leaned on the doorway to the sitting room, watching in silence as Bert scrambled up, deflated and blustering. "That dog's a menace. He needs putting down." He shot a venomous look at Elaine. "And you just wait 'til I get you home."

"I won't be coming home, Albert Parsons. Not tonight, and not ever again."

Max gripped Bert's jacket and turned the man to face him. He grabbed both lapels and tugged, forcing Bert on to his toes. Their noses almost touched. "You'd better leave, Parsons, or you'll be the one that gets hurt."

Bert looked from Max to Libby. "So that's what you're up to, Max Ramshore." His words were slurred. "Got a new woman in town. Well, you're welcome to the ugly cow." He shook off Max's grip and lurched down the path, stumbling and muttering.

Libby held out her hand, struggling to stop it trembling. "That was good timing, Max. Come on in and join the party." She stretched the meal to four, adding extra salad leaves, cutting chicken breasts in half, slicing chunks from a loaf of Frank's finest rustic bread, and opening another bottle of wine.

They ate in the kitchen. Bear settled down to mangle a dog chew; a gentle giant once more. The cat was nowhere to be seen. Elaine, shaking with reaction, refused to go to Accident and Emergency or call the police, but swallowed aspirin and let Mandy lead her upstairs to make up a bed. "I'll go to my sister's in Bristol, on Monday. Bert won't come back tomorrow, not while the dog's here. And not if it means losing drinking time."

Libby stacked plates in the dishwasher. "Now, Max, why are you back so soon, and what did you find out?"

He insisted on making coffee, talking loudly over the grinder and frothing milk with enthusiasm. "Well, I heard about poor old Mrs Thomson. It looks like all the action's over here after all. Why are you laughing?"

"Mrs Thomson told me your name's really Maxwell."

"Anyway," he glared, "I was worried about you. I wasn't sure how you and Bear would get on, after that unfortunate affair with your car. I can see I needn't have worried."

He stretched out in an armchair. "That was a wonderful meal, by the way: better than a restaurant." Fuzzy appeared from his hiding place behind the settee, stretched and sauntered over to

125

sit on Max's knee.

"Thanks. The car's been fixed and Bear's looked after me. He's even made friends with the cat. I'll tell you about Guy Miles and James Sutcliffe in a minute, but first, what did you find out in America?"

"I didn't take to our friend Mickey, that's for sure. Too rich for his own good, that one, with a trophy wife, a mansion in Beverley Hills and a great opinion of himself."

"Did you see his house?"

Max laughed. "No, he graciously offered me half an hour of his time in a hotel. But I'd hired a car, so I did a little snooping around the area. You know, see how the other half live?"

"And?"

"You know, I never would have thought I'd say it, but the heat was too much for me. It's good to get back to some Somerset weather."

Libby shivered. "Gales and rain, you mean. I suppose, at least we don't need air conditioning. Anyway, was Mickey what we expected?"

"Exactly so. I met his wife, by the way. Maybe you've seen her? She's starring in that sci-fi blockbuster that came out last month, and she was giving interviews at the same hotel. Mickey whisked me in and out of the room. I think he was trying to impress me."

"Hm. So, he was rattled?"

"Hard to tell. Trouble is, he's got a great alibi. He spent most of Monday night at a televised award ceremony. Even with the time difference, he couldn't have attacked Susie and got back to the States in time. In any case, he hasn't really got any reason to want her dead, what with the sparkly new wife and all." He peered into Libby's face. "Why are you looking like the cat who got the cream?"

Libby took a moment to savour her triumph. She curled her legs up on the settee. "I just found out today that he and Susie were never divorced. If that film star thinks their wedding was genuine, she's in for a disappointment. He's a bigamist."

The news stunned Max into open-mouthed silence. Then, he threw back his head and laughed. Libby struggled to keep the triumph from showing in her face, as she filled him in with the day's events. "Why didn't you tell me Susie was from a traveller's family?"

"Didn't seem relevant. She lived with her mother, and I knew Alice Bennett died."

"Well, it matters. That's why she didn't like official documents and solicitors. Why she didn't make a will."

Max grunted. "Plenty of people don't make wills. Susie wouldn't have cared where her money went, once her little girl was gone."

"But, if she didn't bother to make a will, and she never divorced Mickey, then he has the best possible motive for having her killed."

"Money? You really think that's what it's about?"

"Why not. Aren't most murders committed for money?"

Max removed Fuzzy from his knee and poked at the logs on the fire, prodding until flames shot up the chimney. "There are plenty of reasons people kill each other. Money, of course, but then there's jealousy, and revenge, and sex crops up, too, pretty often."

Libby clicked her tongue. "Well, what's your theory, then?"

Fuzzy stretched and turned a complete circle, yawned and subsided, eyes fixed on the fire. Max waved one hand. "No theory, yet, but plenty of questions. I think we should keep an open mind. Anyway, you look tired out. Let's leave it for now."

CHAPTER TWENTY-TWO

The Other Lighthouse

Mandy and Elaine slept in on Sunday morning. Libby enjoyed a quiet breakfast with Bear and Fuzzy. She'd see Max again, today. Her stomach performed an odd little flip. Exham had suddenly become a much more interesting place.

They'd arranged to meet in the Lighthouse Inn for Sunday lunchtime drinks. The venue seemed appropriate. Determined not to make too much effort, Libby wore a minimum of makeup: just mascara and lipstick, with the slightest blush of pink on her cheeks. Well, she excused herself, no need to go around looking tired. She pulled on jeans and a raspberry-coloured sweater, brushed her hair until it shone and shrugged on a light grey jacket.

The pub was crowded with pre-dinner drinkers. Libby recognised some of them. Samantha Watson was in the corner, head bent close to Chief Inspector Arnold. She waved a limp hand in the air, without meeting Libby's eyes. "We must have lunch, some time, Libby dear."

Max leaned on the bar, an air-force blue sweater picking up the colour of his eyes. Libby slid onto a stool. "Why did you want to meet here?"

"I thought we should talk to a few of Susie's old friends. See who you recognise from Mrs Thomson's photos."

He hadn't asked her out to enjoy her sparkling wit, then. Libby slipped the Christmas photo onto the bar. "Mrs Thomson told me some of the names. The full names, of course. No nicknames. I wonder if Bert still answers to Albert?" She pointed to one of the boys in the picture, "Who's that, with black hair?"

"That's Chief Inspector Arnold."

Libby snorted. "He's changed a bit. I suppose the beard makes a difference, and the thinning hair. Everyone's changed since this was taken, but I can recognise you. You're just the same."

"Apart from the wrinkles."

"I guess Bert won't be coming in today?"

"Don't bet on it. He'll be looking for sympathy. He thinks he's untouchable. There he is, with Alan and Ned." The garage owner waved. Ned winked. Bert kept his eyes on his shoes.

Samantha, elegant in tight white jeans and a navy cashmere sweater, looking years younger than her age, with not a trace of grey showing through expensive highlights, left the inspector and shimmied over to kiss Max on both cheeks. "Libby and I know each other." Her eyes picked out every detail of Libby's appearance, before she turned her attention to Max, eyelashes aflutter. "We're in the history society together."

Max grinned. "History society. Really?"

"One has to find something to do, here." Samantha heaved a heavy sigh. "It's not Bath, you know." Her voice held a bleak note and a little of Libby's antagonism drained away. Samantha had no children. Libby's two had left home, but they phoned regularly. Lately, she even seemed to have a surrogate child in Mandy, but Samantha, with her lovely face and figure, and lucrative career, was sad, bored and lonely. Ned joined them at the bar, but his wife's lip curled in contempt.

Ollie slid his pint mug along the bar. "Is there a date for Susie's funeral, yet?"

Max shrugged. "Not until the police release her body."

"Your lad Joe was round at our place," Ollie went on. "Asking whether we'd seen her lately."

Samantha tossed her head. "She pretty well walked away from us all when she was famous."

"She was back recently." Libby spoke without thinking. Max glared, sending her a silent message. Maybe she'd stolen his thunder. Samantha blinked. In a flash of inspiration, Libby realised why she looked so young. *Botox*.

Ollie frowned. "Susie was back here? When? Did anyone see her?"

"She went to visit a member of the band. James Sutcliffe's a farmer, now, making cheese, out in the sticks beyond Bristol. Susie came back to visit his wife before she died."

Ollie whistled. "Phew, wish we'd known. Could have had a reunion."

Samantha put a hand on his arm. "I don't think Susie would want to be seen with us, these days, Ollie."

Libby felt an absurd need to defend Susie. "She kept in touch with Mrs Thomson over the years, you know, sending photos."

Samantha's tinkling laugh jarred on Libby's ears. "I don't know why Susie would bother with that nosy old woman. Such a busybody."

Max's eyes flashed steel. "Haven't you heard?"

"Heard what? I've been away the past few days. I only got back from London yesterday." Samantha was very close to Max, her elbow almost touching his.

He took a step away. "Mrs Thomson's dead. She fell down the stairs."

"Oh." Samantha recoiled. "Well, how would I know that? Anyway, it's true, she was a busybody, standing at that window of hers, spying on us all.

She used to tell tales to my parents." She looked round the circle of appalled faces and her voice changed. "It's very sad, all the same."

Libby said. "Anyway, she seems to be the only one in Exham that Susie told about her—" She broke off as Max repeated the glaring routine. She coughed. "About her visit."

Max took her arm. "If we're going to do that walk, Libby, we'd better get going. Joe will let us know as soon as there's a date for the funeral; either of the funerals."

CHAPTER TWENTY-THREE

The Knoll

Libby's back tingled as they walked away. She could swear Samantha's eyes never left her. She hissed, "What was that all about, Max?"

He grinned. "I wanted to see some reactions."

"Not about Susie's daughter, though. That was what you stopped me saying, wasn't it?"

"I thought we should keep that under wraps for a while."

She waited, but he seemed in no hurry to explain. "OK, Max. What aren't you telling me?"

"Let's get out of here, first."

Ten minutes later, they arrived at the foot of the Knoll. Max let Bear out of the car. He jumped up, panting at the prospect of a walk. Libby wasn't so sure. The hill was steep. "You said we were having lunch."

"We'll do a round trip and finish up back at the pub, when everyone's left. We don't want half the town eavesdropping."

She shrugged and set off. "Then, why did we come to a pub where you knew we'd find all your school friends?"

"Told you: for reactions. Like Samantha's. What did she have against Mrs Thomson?"

"Or against Susie?" Libby shot a glance his way. "Max, why didn't you let me tell them about Annie Rose?" The hill grew steeper. Max's legs were long and Libby found it hard to match his stride. "Can't we slow down a bit?"

"What? Oh, all right." He slowed the pace a tiny fraction.

"You're blushing, Max. Come on, spill the beans. I thought we were supposed to be partners." She was tired of wondering about Max's history. A hint here, a tiny piece of information there: he was so secretive. "What happened with you and Susie, when you were growing up together?"

"Susie and I were good friends, back in the day. Before she left school. I suppose you'd call us childhood sweethearts."

"And Samantha was jealous."

He chuckled. "A bit, maybe. Susie and I were together for over a year. She was a dear, sweet girl. At first, anyway. Then, the band took off and things changed. She got drunk too often, even for a teenager. She started smoking pot. Everyone was doing it in those days, but when Susie got high, she was wild. She didn't seem to know when to

135

stop."

"I suppose it's easy to get carried away, if you're in a successful band." Libby panted, struggling to keep up as Max climbed faster.

"Guy didn't go to our school. He was at a public school nearby: his father was a wealthy man. Guy kept Susie supplied, not only with pot, but LSD and then coke, later. I was more jealous than shocked, if I'm honest, because she spent more time with Guy than with me. I suppose I could see the writing on the wall."

Max's face took on a far-away look, as though he was reliving the past: a past when he was in love with Susie. "One day we had an argument." He breathed hard, from walking and talking, and slowed his pace to let Libby catch up. "Susie had a Saturday job in the newsagents. One afternoon, I went in to get cigarettes."

He glanced sideways, caught Libby's eye and grimaced. "Everyone smoked, back then. The owner went into the back room. When Susie put my money in the till, she lifted a handful of cash. It wasn't much, but it gave me a jolt. We had a row, and I accused her of being a drug addict. She laughed at me."

Max bent over, picked up a handful of stones and tossed them into a hollow. "She said: 'You go around with your eyes shut, Max. If you only knew...' I had no idea what she was talking about. I suppose I was a bit dim, in those days. I wouldn't let it go. I got mad, accused her of preferring Guy to me, of sleeping with him. She just roared with laughter and I stormed off. Neither of us apologised and we broke up. That's it, really. An everyday story of teenagers."

Libby stopped walking. "But, you must have known she wasn't sleeping with Guy."

"What? Of course, she was. She didn't deny it."

"Max, he's gay. I told you, he's living with Alvin. They're a couple."

"You're kidding." He scratched his head. "Guy? Who'd have thought it? Are you sure?"

She nodded. He gave a crack of laughter. "More fool me. Well, Susie and I didn't get back together." He stopped, frowning, as though thinking hard. He murmured, "Not Guy? Then who?" He shrugged. "Well, the band played at Glastonbury, Mickey came along, whisked her off to the States and married her."

Libby's head was spinning. "Can we sit down for a bit?"

They perched on a couple of the stones that speckled the hillside, and Libby's heart rate slowed to something more normal as she gazed out across a patchwork of fields. Rooks swooped, cawing, high above. The wind blew Max's hair over his eyes and he shoved it back with an impatient hand.

Of course, Max still had a soft spot for Susie, his first love. It was touching, really. Those teenage years, when life was so intense. That must have been around the time Libby met Trevor. She shook the thought away and spoke lightly. "Well, that's quite a story. I guess we all have stuff in our past. Anyway, did you see Susie again after she left the country?"

"No. I was too proud. I wasn't going to chase after her. I wish I had. Not to get back together again, just to keep an eye on her. She could have used some old friends, I think."

"My mother used to say, 'If wishes were horses then beggars would ride.' Come on, I'll race you to the top."

Max overtook Libby easily. She stood and watched as he climbed on, towards the summit. What were those motives he'd mentioned? Money, jealousy, revenge, sex. Max could have nursed his anger at Susie all these years, and seized the opportunity for revenge when she came back.

He turned to wait for Libby, and she remembered he'd been gone when Mrs Thomson was killed. Relief left her legs shaky. She closed her eyes for a moment. She'd been in danger of letting imagination run away with her. She put on a spurt of speed and caught up with him.

Bear reached the summit first. He rolled in a patch of hazy sunshine. Max reached back to pull Libby, panting, up the last few yards. She groaned. "I need to get into shape."

"You look good enough to me." She blinked, surprised, and a little warm glow ignited inside.

He was still talking. "I've been thinking about Mickey."

The autumn sun warmed Libby's face as she leaned her back against the jutting rock. "Sorry, what did you say?"

"Mickey. You were right. I'd crossed him off the list of suspects. His alibi's pretty unshakeable, it's true, but Susie put a lot of money away in the bank for Annie Rose. If he knew about that, it would be a big motive, like you said. A man like him wouldn't need to come over and murder her himself. He'd outsource it."

It was probably as close as Max ever came to an apology. "He probably knows plenty of criminals. Even if he didn't know any English hitmen, they could come across from the US."

The sun went behind a cloud and Libby shivered. "You've been asking Mickey questions. He'll know you suspect him."

"But he doesn't know you found out about the missing divorce. Who does?"

"Well, James Sutcliffe showed me a letter she'd

sent. They kept in touch, you know. I didn't tell anyone else. Or did I? I wish I could remember…"

"Take it easy. It'll come back to you if you don't think too hard. We need to keep it as quiet as we can. If Mickey knew Susie was in the UK, he must have had people watching her. They may still be around. We don't want them to know what we suspect."

She grabbed his arm. "Max, I told Mandy."

He groaned. "Then it will be all over town. Libby, take care. Look what happened to Mrs Thomson. I'll leave Bear with you for a while. He'll look after you. Keep your eyes open and don't go out alone, especially at night."

CHAPTER TWENTY-FOUR

Diary

A weak autumn sun shone above Exham next morning. Cold dread had haunted Libby after the conversation with Max, but it evaporated with the night. Of course, she was in no danger. They'd been over-dramatising.

She hummed as she showered and dressed. She drove Mandy and Elaine to the station, on the first leg of their journey to Bristol, waving as they crossed the bridge. Mandy planned to stay, settling her mother in with her aunt, before returning in a day or so. "I'll try to get Mum to talk to the police." Mandy had a determined glint in her eye.

Libby planned to take Bear back to Max. She'd kept him here for one last night, but there was no space in her tiny house for such an enormous animal. He needed to run free on Max's extensive grounds. "Make the most of it," she told Fuzzy. She gathered up the day's post from the mat. "We're both going to miss that dog."

She flipped through the handful of letters: a catalogue, two flyers and something official from

Trevor's solicitor. More on the slow progress of probate, presumably. It seemed to take forever, even though he'd left everything to Libby.

She ripped the letter open. *Dear Mrs Forest...* She sank on to the bottom stair, deaf to the racket Fuzzy and Bear made, chasing one another round the house. The letter shook in her hand. Nausea gripped her stomach.

She read the words again, hoping she'd misunderstood. *We regret to inform you...* The solicitor used careful, legal language, but the meaning was clear. There was no money. Trevor had spent every penny, and more. He'd had accounts in places Libby had never dreamed about, all with overdrafts and loans. The solicitor had tracked them all down, paid back as many as possible and set out the account for Libby to see.

Trevor's debts far exceeded the total of the estate. Libby was broke. What's more, she owed several thousand pounds to Trevor's creditors. Shaky, she heaved her body up. A headache tightened its grip on both temples. She threw the letter on the kitchen counter, mechanically spooned instant coffee into a mug, searched for aspirin and wondered what in the world she was going to do.

It was already late. She had to go to work. She couldn't afford to lose the job: in fact, she'd have to ask Frank for more hours. She brushed her hair and found a coat. Released from paralysis, her mind buzzed. The business course would have to wait. Thank heaven, she'd sold the London house. It had been in both names. Trevor had slipped up, there. This house had been much cheaper, so Libby had some funds in her bank account, but not many. Would they be enough?

The advance from the book publisher was tiny. It wouldn't keep her for long. She'd better finish the work. Susie's death had taken over Libby's life, this past week. She'd become obsessed with Susie, Mrs Thomson and Max. She needed to sort out her life.

The morning at the bakery passed in a fog. Business had returned to normal; the excitement over Susie's death little more than a nine-day wonder. Libby could hardly talk, for the knot in her stomach. She had no clear idea, afterwards, who she'd spoken to or what she'd said. She'd ask Frank about extra work tomorrow. She'd burst into tears if she tried to broach the subject today.

She left as soon as her shift ended and drove home, where Bear and Fuzzy snored, curled together in a bundle of fur, in Bear's apple crate. Libby started the computer. She'd experimented enough with recipes. It was time to write them up. She worked for two hours, hardly glancing away from the keyboard, except to check her notes.

Finally, she stretched. Her shoulders ached and a lump of cement seemed to have settled in her stomach. She couldn't eat, even though she'd had no lunch. She'd suck a mint: that might help. She pulled out the drawer where she kept a supply.

Mrs Thomson's papers lay on top of the tin. Not now. Libby slammed the drawer shut. There was no time to think about Mrs Thomson. She had a living to earn. She'd leave the police and Max to find out what happened to Susie and the old lady.

She leaned both elbows on the desk, hardly noticing as the cursor winked. It was no good. She couldn't concentrate on the book anymore. A surge of guilt had brought on a cold sweat. She'd stolen Mrs Thomson's papers, hiding clues from the police. She ought to hand them over.

Libby groaned. She couldn't do it. The police would stuff the papers in a file and forget them, but someone drowned Susie and pushed Mrs Thomson downstairs, and they thought they'd got away with it. Libby meant to prove they were wrong.

She cleared a space on the desk, lifted the heap of papers and books from the drawer, and laid everything in a neat pile. She set the photograph album aside, flipped open a blue, hardback book and ran a finger down one line after another of small, crabbed handwriting. Each page was dated, like a diary. Libby chose a page at random.

Monday 15 March

2.30pm Judy Roach took her three boys down to the beach. They walked all the way to the lighthouse. Philip had a new, red bucket, and made sandcastles, but his older brothers kicked them down.

7pm Five girls were running wild on the beach this evening. They collected driftwood and tried to light a bonfire but the wood was wet. Do their parents know what they're up to?

So far, so dull. An everyday story of a sleepy seaside town after the summer visitors had left. *Wait.* A sudden brainwave set Libby's pulse racing. She turned to the back of the book, fingers fumbling. What if Mrs Thomson saw what happened on the day Susie died? Maybe she'd recorded it here, in the dairy.

Libby checked the dates on the final pages. The notes stopped the day before Susie's death. Disappointment kicked in. Libby tossed the book on the desk and trailed down to make tea, narrowly escaping a fall as Fuzzy appeared in front of her, from nowhere. "Hello. You're friendly, today. Bear's having a good effect on you."

She picked the cat up to stroke the soft fur. "If you've been wondering what's going on, Fuzz,

145

you're not the only one." Bear snored in the apple crate, twitching, dreaming of bones, or chasing rabbits. With a sudden wail, Fuzzy leaped from Libby's arms and ran up the stairs, into the study, onto the desk.

"Watch out." Libby grabbed the cat's tail as papers slithered across the surface, on to the floor. Fuzzy settled on the shambles and purred. "Oh, they smell of Bear, do they? Is that what you're telling me? Well, I'll be finished with them, soon. There aren't any clues there, after all."

Libby retrieved sheets of paper from the floor and tapped them into a neat pile. She glanced at the bundle in her hands. Just a spiral-bound notepad and a few clean, detached sheets. She flicked through the pad. It was blank. She set it aside, turning to one of the loose pages. The light from the computer monitor reflected back from the paper. Libby squinted. She could see indentations—the kind left by pressure from a pen.

She flipped through the pile, a faint spark of hope flickering, only to die a moment later. There was no sign of the top sheet. Frustrated, Libby grabbed the indented page and held it up to the light. Was that an S? She peered more closely. Yes, and those marks were W and E. Try as she might, though, Libby failed to make out any full words.

The doorbell interrupted her train of thought.

Annoyed, she weighed down loose pages with the tin of mints, scooped up the cat and wandered downstairs to open the door. Max leaned on the doorstep.

CHAPTER TWENTY-FIVE

Rubbish

"I came to say you should hang on to Bear, until this business is over. He'll keep you safe."

Libby, not listening, grabbed Max's arm and tugged him inside the house. "Never mind that, now. Follow me." She led him upstairs, protesting. "Look. Can you see?"

She thrust the blue notebook under Max's nose. He squinted. "Not really."

"These are Mrs Thomson's notes. She watched from the window, writing about everything she saw, then transcribed everything into her diary."

Understanding lit Max's eyes as he read the short entries. "These are from the week before Susie died." He flipped to the end. "Oh—"

"I know. The last day's missing. It's not there—" Excitement made Libby babble. She took a breath. "At first, I thought Mrs Thomson hadn't been watching the beach that day, but then I saw these marks. The top page has gone, but you can make out some of the letters, where she pressed down."

"Why would the top sheet be missing?"

Libby drew a sharp breath. "Oh. Do you think the – the killer took them?"

Max's eyes narrowed. "You could be right. We have to know what she wrote. The police can read it: they have specialist equipment. We'll take all this to Joe." He waved a hand at the papers.

"Oh." It was an anti-climax. Libby murmured, "Can't we try to understand it ourselves?"

Max laughed. "You're not a fan of the police, I take it. Well, since they're convinced Mrs Thomson's death was an accident, I don't suppose they'll be in any hurry to look at her notes. How did you get these, by the way?"

Libby's face burned. "I suppose I stole them from Mrs Thomson's house."

"Did you, indeed." Max twinkled. "Well, before we confess to my son, who'll make a song and dance about it, let's see what we can find out." Taking a lead pencil from the pot on Libby's desk, Max rubbed lightly over the surface of the paper. The indentations stood out clearly against the dark background. "You still can't see all the letters, but there should be enough to tell us if it's useful."

Libby, leaning over his shoulder, grabbed a sheet of copy paper and wrote: *4 J. boys' castles. 5 rain. 5.15 T. walking L. 6 Windy, wet. B rubbish. 7 Tide.* "I think that's right. I've had to guess at some of the words. It still doesn't make much sense."

Max grinned. "It's Mrs Thomson's own shorthand. All we have to do is crack the code. How are you with crosswords?" He reached over the table. "Maybe the diary will help." He opened the blue notebook and, heads together, they pored over the pages. "Look. You see? In this entry, she's made a note of the time of day. That's what the numbers mean."

Libby pointed to the entry she'd read earlier. "I bet the J is Judy Roach. She walks on the beach with her three boys and they build sandcastles."

"There you are, then. Well done. Now, there are also notes on the weather: wet, windy and so on. We can use those to check which day Mrs Thomson's talking about." Max grinned. "I've got an app." Libby hid a smile. Her son had a phone full of apps.

Max fiddled with his mobile. "There, you were right. Mrs Thomson made these notes on the day Susie died."

His words bumped Libby back to earth. For a moment, she'd forgotten this was about murder.

Max scrolled down the page, comparing times. "We can read most of it. At 5 o'clock, it started to rain. A quarter of an hour later, T was walking L—a dog, I suppose. We should be able to find who that was easily enough."

Libby remembered. "Thelma Hunt has a dog called Lily. I've seen them on the beach when I walk Shipley."

Max frowned. "Shipley?"

"He's the dog I walk for Marina. It's not important."

"Right. Ever thought of getting your own dog?" Max turned back to the code. "At 6 o'clock it was windy and wet. B must be another name, but what does *rubbish* mean?" Libby shook her head.

Max waved the problem away. "Never mind. We can come back to that. There's just one entry left. At 7 o'clock, she wrote *tide*. I guess she means high tide. It came right in, that night." He straightened up, rubbing his back. "So, just a couple of mysteries left. On the night of Susie's death, Mrs Thomson saw B just as the tide was coming in. B must be a person. I wonder what B was doing. She just wrote *rubbish*."

Libby looked through the notebook, but there was no other entry like that. B must be an initial, like J and T. But why *rubbish*? After an hour, they'd pored over every word in the blue book. There were lots of names beginning with B, but there was no way to know who'd been on the beach, in stormy conditions, on the day Susie died.

Max sucked a mint. "It could be someone who's never appeared in the book before. That

151

would mean they don't often come to the beach. It rules out dog-walkers."

"But Mrs Thomson knew the murderer. She let them into her house. That means it was someone from the town."

Max sat on the edge of the table. "Maybe I'm jumping to conclusions, but I'd be willing to bet Mrs Thomson's *rubbish* meant something like a bag of trash."

Libby shivered. "A black bag, you mean? Susie wasn't in a bag when I found her."

"No, the tide could have ripped the bag away, if it wasn't securely tied. It's fierce at this time of year."

Libby remembered the missing boot. The storm tide had enough strength to wrench a leather boot from Susie's foot. It could easily dispose of thin black plastic. She bit her lip. "So, B was the killer."

"We'd better ring the police."

CHAPTER TWENTY-SIX

Balancing the Books

Detective Sergeant Joe Ramshore scolded Libby for interfering with a police investigation, as if she were a naughty schoolgirl. Max's involvement infuriated him even more. "You're not above the law, either of you," he snapped.

Eventually, he agreed not to charge her, going so far as to promise a check on every B on the electoral register for the town. "You see, it's the day-to-day police work that will solve this, Mrs Forest, not amateur dabbling." Libby kept her temper in check, fighting the urge to point out he'd wasted days refusing to believe Mrs Thomson's death was suspicious.

She phoned Ned, the builder, to explain she couldn't afford to go ahead with the alterations to the bathroom. "Don't you worry about it, Mrs F. I'll keep the plans we made, and you let me know as soon as you want to go ahead." Libby felt dreadful. That was the trouble with a small town: you knew and liked the people who worked for you.

She wrote to the solicitor, suggesting ways of sorting out the mess of Trevor's debts. Then, needing a break, she went to the local history group meeting. The group reviewed last week's event at the Hall. "It was a huge success." Angela was the treasurer. "We split the profits with the Hall, and we've made enough to pay for a year's worth of speakers. Not that we don't have some excellent ones of our own." She smiled at Beryl, in the corner, fingering a stack of notes. "Everyone loved Marina's talk."

"I thought I'd die when Libby was down to her shift," There was a ripple of laughter. Libby had almost forgotten those awful Victorian clothes. There were so many layers. She frowned. A thought tugged at the back of her mind, but she couldn't get hold of it. It was about the costume. Or, was it? She concentrated, but she couldn't recall. Oh well, maybe it would come back to her.

Susie's funeral was set for Thursday afternoon and Mandy returned from Bristol, where she'd stayed with her mother and aunt, the evening before. She insisted on making dinner, using one of Libby's recipes for a sausage casserole. "Oh, it's so good to be back. They drive me mad, those two. Always on at me for my tats, and the piercings."

Libby kept silent on the subject of the tattoos

that climbed Mandy's arms and encircled her neck. "Mandy, you're old enough to look after yourself. Get a flat."

Mandy blushed and cleared her throat. "I don't suppose you'd like a permanent lodger, would you?"

"I'd love you to live with me, but that's not exactly standing on your own two feet, is it?" *But I could use the cash.*

"I can't afford a proper flat of my own."

"Well, in that case. Just for a while."

With a spurt of hard work that lasted well into the small hours of every morning, Libby had written three quarters of the cookery book. Frank had taken her on full-time. He'd even given her a raise and a new job title: Development Consultant.

She still felt sick at the thought of the money Trevor owed. The bathroom made her want to cry, with its bright orange tiles; a shower that dripped slow, barely-warm water; and a cracked window. She'd have to live with it for at least another year. She could almost believe Trevor had planned it all out of spite: a final insult from beyond the grave. Libby would work her socks off to get free of him.

The evening was dark and still. She stood at the window of her study and stretched, muscles tense from an hour at the computer. There was so little light here. Stars filled the whole expanse of sky. Maybe she'd get a telescope, one day in the far future, when she'd cleared the debts, and learn more about them.

The street lay deserted. Only one car passed, turning into a nearby driveway, the engine dying. Libby heard the clunk of a garage door. She opened the window to smell the sea and took a deep breath. This beat London's bright lights.

A movement on the left caught her attention. Instinctively, she drew back, inside the window, as a figure crept, soundless, close to the wall of the house, around the corner and past the sycamore tree, finally disappearing into shadow. That was odd. Libby didn't expect a visitor. Ears straining, she listened for a knock on the door, but all was quiet. She slipped downstairs and hovered, just inside the front door, watching through the tiny pane of glass, but there was no sign of a caller.

Uneasy, heart pounding, she crept past the sitting room, where Mandy was watching a game show, into the kitchen. The curtains and blinds were drawn tight against the autumn night. With a clatter, Bear brushed past, almost knocking Libby off her feet as he leaped at the back door, barking, the noise battering Libby's ears. He'd heard a sound, too. Libby scrambled to the door, fumbling with the lock, and flung it open.

There was no one there. One hand on the dog, the other clenched tight, Libby stepped outside. The air was cool and still. She sniffed. Was that a whiff of beer? She hadn't imagined it, then. Someone had been here.

She tiptoed round the side of the house and back again. The stalker was long gone. In the distance, a car engine revved and faded. Mandy was at the back door. "What was all that about? I heard Bear going crazy."

Libby hesitated. Mandy needed to be on her guard. She shrugged. "I thought someone was outside."

"Who'd be creeping about in the dark?"

"I don't know." She locked the door, shaking it to check it was secure, sat Mandy down and told her what they'd found in Mrs Thomson's diary. "Maybe whoever was sneaking around knew I took it from her house." Someone at the police station had blabbed.

"It's a good thing Bear's staying." Mandy seemed unfazed. "He won't let anyone near."

Libby lay awake for a long time, that night, chills running up and down her spine. If the stalker was the same person who'd pushed Mrs Thomson down the stairs, both she and Mandy were in danger.

Her brain whirled, images chasing each other in

a confused kaleidoscope of the past days. There was Susie, slumped under the lighthouse like a sack of rubbish; Mrs Thomson, gazing out of her window at a world that passed her by; the local history group, gossiping; the "Band of Brothers" of local men, looking to Max for guidance; James Sutcliffe and Guy each living a new life as though the wild days of the band never happened.

In her mind's eye, Libby recalled the pictures of Susie, with Mickey on her wedding day, and of her daughter, Annie Rose. Sleep wouldn't come, now. Libby pushed back the duvet, thrust cold feet into slippers and softly, so as not to wake Mandy, slipped along to the study. She grabbed a clean, fresh sheet of copy paper and began to write.

CHAPTER TWENTY-SEVEN

Funeral

The weather forecast for Susie's funeral promised a day of cold, watery sunshine. Libby, torn between an old grey trench coat and the long, formal, black wool coat she'd bought for Trevor's funeral, peered anxiously at the sky. "I'll wear the wool coat, otherwise I might never use it again." She winced as Mandy, appropriate for once in her customary head-to-toe black, fiddled with her latest piercing, at the top of one ear. "Doesn't that hurt?"

At the church, Max squeezed Libby's arm. "Every shop in town must be shut." The town streamed in, past a phalanx of photographers. "Even the national newspapers are here. Pity Susie isn't around to enjoy it."

"There's Guy." Guy brushed past the photographers, eyes straight ahead. Alvin stopped to flick a speck of dust off his jacket. James Sutcliffe was there, too, his son steering him past the press who were, in any case, far too busy interviewing Samantha to notice the once famous members of Susie's band. Tossing her fringe, one elegant foot in front of the other, Samantha nailed, with ease, the self-appointed role of Susie's best friend.

As the service ended, Susie's own voice swelled through speakers, echoing around the Church. James Sutcliffe blew his nose. A lump lodged in Libby's throat.

The local hotel, run by Marina's sister, put on a spread, the garden bathed in Indian summer sunshine. Libby, glass juggled in one hand, plate balanced on an old stone wall, reached into her shoulder bag for the paper she'd worked on all night. "Here, Max, I think you should read this."

He took the document, narrowed eyes fierce on her face. "What's this about, Libby?"

"Read it. Tell me if I'm wrong."

Max ran his eyes down the page. Expression stony, he flicked a glance at Libby, folded the sheet of paper into a neat square, and tucked it into an inside jacket pocket. "Well done. Very clever, Mrs Forest."

Before she could answer, a black, stretch limousine screeched to a halt outside the hotel. The uniformed chauffeur leaped out to fling open a rear door and a middle-aged man eased from the car, long grey hair caught in a ponytail. Gold earrings flashed and a medallion sparkled at the neck of his open-collar black silk shirt. Max murmured, "There he is: Mickey Garston himself."

Two thick-set men, startling with shaved heads and earpieces, leaped from a second car and took up positions close behind Mickey, eyes hidden by reflective sunglasses. Mandy let out a low whistle. Mickey's transatlantic accent, loud enough to rattle glasses on the wooden tables dotted around the hotel garden, boomed over the crowd. "Hey, I guess I missed the funeral. That's too bad. Caught up in your English traffic."

Max's mouth was close to Libby's ear. "What do you think he's here for?"

The newcomer stretched out an arm. "Max, my old buddy, good to see you again." He grabbed Max's hand, the other arm snaking round his neck. "Won't you introduce me to Susie's friends?"

Max extricated himself, unsmiling. "I see you came, after all."

"Max, my friend, introduce me. Who's this gorgeous creature?" Samantha, white teeth flashing, poised on four-inch stiletto heels. She extended one graceful arm, tinkling with bracelets, to take the flabby hand.

Lightbulbs popped. Bored journalists set down half-eaten sausage rolls, flipped their note pads to new pages and pulled out cheap biros. A hoarse bellow splintered the air. "What the hell are you doing here?" James Sutcliffe, fists raised, elbowed past Libby. "Get back to the pond you crawled out of."

Mickey's bodyguards rearranged themselves on either side of the boss. Max's single step dissected the space between Sutcliffe and the Americans. Jack Sutcliffe grasped his father's arm. "Come away, Dad, it's too late for that. Leave it."

Sutcliffe shook the arm away, his face purple. "You've got a nerve, Garston, showing your face here after what you did."

Mickey flinched. "Come on now, no need for this. I'm just paying my respects—"

James Sutcliffe shook his fist. "You killed Susie's little girl."

Mickey swallowed. He raised his hands, palms out, bluster gone. "No need for that, now." He frowned. "James Sutcliffe? Is that really you? After all these years?" He let his hands fall. "Now, come on, man. It wasn't my fault the kid died. Why, I was as upset as anyone."

Sutcliffe's voice shook. "Susie trusted Annie Rose with you, just for one day. All you had to do was play with the child, and keep her safe. So what did you do?" He clenched his fists. Tears wetted the weather-beaten cheeks. "You sat in front of the TV, drinking beer and eating fast food like a

162

pig. How long was she in the pool, dead, before you even noticed she'd gone?"

Mickey shifted, edging backwards towards the car. "Come on, now. The kid could swim. She was playing with her dog. I guess he jumped in and she followed. It wasn't my fault." He shrugged. "Susie had no right to leave the kid with me, anyway. She wasn't even mine."

"Not yours? What do you mean, not yours?"

Mickey laughed through twisted lips. "You still don't know, do you? Susie managed to fool us all. She sure made a monkey out of me. Yes, your precious Susie Bennett was already pregnant when we met. She tried to pass the baby off as premature and told me it was mine."

Someone gasped. Guy's face creased in a frown. Then, he shattered the stunned silence. "Do you remember, James? That summer, at Glastonbury, Susie wasn't well. She was sick every day."

"That was because of the mud." James Sutcliffe shrugged. "It rained so hard, that year, there was mud everywhere. Couldn't get away from it. Slept in it, sat in it. It got into the food, the beer. In the end, we gave up trying to keep clean. People were ill, plenty of 'em, not just Susie. Caught things from the bacteria in the mud."

"And we thought Susie caught a bug." Guy pushed his glasses up his nose. "But, maybe we were wrong. Maybe she was sick because she was pregnant."

Max joined in. "Susie left town suddenly, after Glastonbury. No one expected it."

Guy shrugged. "She was so excited about our big break. She couldn't wait to get over to the States. She left with him," he gestured at Mickey, "and we followed a few weeks later."

Libby studied the puzzled faces of Susie's old school mates. Most registered shock and surprise—but not quite all. A bubble of excitement grew inside Libby's chest. "You all knew Susie, you'd grown up with her, but she didn't trust anyone with her secret." One pair of eyes slid away.

Mickey folded his arms. "Yeah. She was expecting someone else's baby, and she kept it a secret until after she'd got me up the aisle." His lips twisted. "She thought she was so clever, putting one over on me. But I'm no fool. I wouldn't have got where I am, if I couldn't work a few things out. That was no premature baby, I can tell you." He pointed a finger at Guy. "Soon as the kid was born, I put two and two together, and made five. Anyway, Annie Rose looked nothing like me. She had blue eyes. Nobody in my family ever had blue eyes."

He swaggered past the security guards. "I did

right by her. I was straight with her and she made a fool out of me, but even then, I didn't kick her out."

"Course you didn't," Guy jeered. "You were making a fortune out of her—out of us all. She was your meal ticket. Because of Susie, you were rich enough, and powerful enough, to keep the scandal out of the press."

Mickey called to the bodyguards. "Come on, boys, let's get out of here. I came over to pay my respects, and all I get is abuse—"

"Who are you trying to fool, Mickey?" Max said. "You don't care about Susie. You came over here to find out if she left a will. Well, you're in luck. She didn't. You'll go on getting what you always wanted from Susie—money."

Mickey paused, one foot in the limousine. His lip curled in a snarl. "She owed me." The car door slammed.

As the vehicle drew away, a single black cloud scudded across the sky, blotting out the sun. Heavy drops of rain spattered the tables and guests ran for cover. Inside the building, tension suddenly broken, the gossip began. Speculation and questions fizzed through the air.

Guy's voice rose above the others. "If Mickey wasn't Annie Rose's father, then who was?"

165

CHAPTER TWENTY-EIGHT

Wake

Max's spoon clinked against a glass. Slowly, the hubbub died away. "Nearly everyone from the old days is here, today. It's been a shock, I know, for most of us. But not to one of us. Not to the father of Susie's baby."

A murmur almost drowned Max's words. He raised his voice. "Susie never told anyone the child wasn't Mickey's, but she had a plan, just in case he found out. She put money away, for her little girl. It was insurance, in case Mickey found out he'd been tricked into marrying Susie and she was left to provide for the child. She never needed it, because Annie Rose died."

He beckoned to Libby. "Why don't you tell them the rest? You've worked it all out."

Libby cleared her throat. "The person who killed Susie and dumped her body under the lighthouse came from this town." On Libby's left, Mandy clutched her mother's arm, white knuckles bright against Elaine's black jacket. To her right, Susie's old schoolmates clustered together.

Alan Jenkins was scrubbed and clean in his best suit, no trace of oil visible today. Samantha Watson leaned her head close to Chief Inspector Arnold, taking no notice of her husband, Ned, who stood on her other side. Angela, Marina, George and the others from the local history society gazed at Libby, eyes wide. Bert, Elaine's husband, leaned against the wall, on the far side of the room, as far from his wife and daughter as possible.

Guy and the two Sutcliffes, father and son, stood a little apart from the townspeople, while Joe Ramshore leaned against the door, suspicious eyes fixed on Libby. She took a breath. "Susie drowned, just like her daughter. It looked like an accident, or suicide. A woman still grieving for the loss of her daughter: who'd be surprised if she chose the same way to die? She was bruised. Again, you'd expect that, what with the way the sea lashed the shore, on the night she died. It didn't prove she was murdered. But one thing did prove it."

Feet shuffled. A forest of faces goggled at Libby. "You all knew old Mrs Thomson. Lonely, missing her husband, she spent her days watching the world go by. She saw everything that happened on the beach, from her window. Some of you called her a nosy parker."

More than one pair of eyes slid away. "You were right. Mrs Thomson watched what went on, down at the beach, and she kept a diary. She saw the murderer dump the body under the lighthouse, that Monday evening, and she made a note of it. I found some of the notes in her house, but someone had been there before me. That person shoved the old lady down the stairs and took the notes."

In the sudden hubbub, Joe Ramshore pushed himself away from the door and cleared his throat. Libby shook her head. "Luckily, the police didn't lock me up for removing the evidence. The notes were missing, but the murderer left behind the second sheet of paper from the pad, and we could make out the words." Someone gasped. "Unfortunately, they were in Mrs Thomson's own brand of shorthand and she didn't write the full name of the murderer."

"Well," Samantha said. "In that case, we're no further forward." Her voice rang with disdain. "Perhaps you should leave the investigation to the police, Libby. After all, they know the town. You've only lived here five minutes."

"But she's been a good friend to us," Mandy shouted. "Better than you, with your posh clothes and—"

Libby waved a hand. "It's all right, Mandy.

Samantha does have a point. I haven't lived here long, but as an outsider, perhaps I could see what was going on more easily than the rest of you."

She waited for the murmurs to die down. She couldn't care less if people thought she was interfering. Susie deserved justice. "At first, we suspected Susie's husband. Because Susie hadn't bothered with a will, he had a solid financial motive."

Faces brightened. If Mickey was the murderer, everyone else was off the hook. Libby went on, "But why would he wait until she was back in England? Wouldn't it have been far easier to have his wife killed in his own country?"

She had their full attention. "I wanted to know more about Susie. I needed to know what she was like when she lived here, in Exham, where she died. Why was she killed here? Why now, and not sooner, perhaps when she first refused to give Mickey a divorce?"

Libby's throat was dry. She took a sip of water, listening to the awkward shuffle of feet, the sharp intakes of breath. "Everyone I spoke to filled in another part of the jigsaw. I discovered the men here seemed to like Susie, but the women didn't." Someone giggled, and was hushed.

"I heard how Susie left Exham in such a hurry, and I began to wonder why. If she was pregnant, did the father know about the child? That was my next question. What would he do, if he ever found out? Then, I understood. Susie's murder had nothing to do with money, after all. It was about Annie Rose: about children, parents and jealousy."

"Mrs Thomson knew everyone in town, and she recognised the murderer. She saw someone she knew, carrying what looked like a sack of rubbish. That's what got her killed. She'd no idea of the importance of what she saw. When she made her rough notes, she used the initial, as she always did, to remind her when she came to write up the diary."

Libby raised her voice, to make sure everyone in the room heard. "The killer's name begins with B."

She waited. First one head, then another, turned. Every horrified face pointed in the same direction, eyes wide, mouths agape. At last, Alan Jenkins blurted out the name. "Bert Parsons."

CHAPTER TWENTY-NINE

Ancestors

Mandy's mother screamed, the sound muffled by a clenched fist stuffed into her mouth. Bert raised red-rimmed eyes. "It wasn't me, Elaine."

Alan said, "We all know you're not afraid of a spot of violence."

Bert's head flicked from one side to the other, searching in vain for a friendly face. "No-no. I didn't k-kill Susie," he stammered. "I never even went out with her. I was about the only one that didn't. I was already with you, Elaine. You know that. We got married just after we left school."

Elaine ran at her husband, outstretched fingers curled like a cat's. "That doesn't mean you weren't going with Susie at the same time."

"Wait." Max's voice rang out, and Elaine stopped.

Libby said, "Bert seemed a very likely suspect, but I saw a photo of Susie's daughter in Mrs Thomson's album. Annie Rose was very fair, with blonde hair and blue eyes."

"That proves it." Bert pointed at his own head.

He was turning bald, the remaining hair was thin, but it was still dark brown, almost black. His eyes were brown, like Mandy's.

Marina said, "It doesn't prove anything. Susie had blonde hair, so of course Annie Rose did."

"No." Angela stepped forward. "Susie had blonde hair when she was small, but hair often darkens as you get older. Don't you remember, at senior school? Susie's hair began to turn brown when she was about fifteen. She was devastated, and she started dyeing it. All that fair hair came out of a bottle."

Libby raised a hand to interrupt the arguments. "Angela's right. Anyone can dye their hair any colour they choose, but Annie Rose's hair was unusually light in colour, sandy really. What combination of genes would give her such pale hair? And she had very blue eyes. Not green, or hazel, but bright blue. Her colouring doesn't rule Bert out, but maybe he wasn't the only man having an affair with Susie just before she left town."

She looked straight at Samantha. "Tell me, Samantha. What's Ned's real name?"

Samantha's head jerked up, face contorted. "Wh-what do you mean? Ned, his name's Ned."

"No, Samantha." Angela said. "Ned's family thought themselves a cut above the rest of us,

172

descended from ancient Scots and the former owners of the Hall. They wouldn't give their son an ordinary name, like Ned."

Every eye was on Angela. "I remember the day we started primary school, when the teacher took the register for the first time. She read out his name and we all laughed. Ned cried, he was so embarrassed." She put an arm around Samantha's shoulder. "Samantha, my dear, I'm afraid you already know this. Ned's real name is Benedict."

Wild-eyed, face purple, Ned stared from one face to another. With a roar, like an animal in pain, he dashed for the door. Guy stuck out a foot and Ned fell, heavily, on the plush carpet. Samantha said. "Your hair's that pale, sandy colour, or it used to be, before you lost most of it. It's your Scottish family."

Libby said, "Most people had forgotten you were called Benedict, but Mrs Thomson always used full names. To her, you remained Benedict, even when everyone else called you Ned."

Joe Ramshore tightened his grip on one of Ned's arms. Max had grabbed the other, but after that first dash for freedom, Ned gave up the struggle. He was crying, his words muffled by sobs. "I never knew Annie Rose was my baby. Susie should have told me. Samantha and me, we tried for children, but we never had any. It broke

173

my heart, but," he cried louder, "all the time I was a father."

He took a long, shuddering breath. "Susie came back to England, to see Mary Sutcliffe one last time. I bumped into her in Bristol." He wiped his nose on his sleeve. "She still looked the same: still the Susie I'd loved. We met up, just for a drink, one night." He glared at Samantha. "You were out with your fancy man, that policeman, pretending to be at work. You must have thought I was stupid."

Chief Inspector Arnold stepped closer to Samantha. Ned's lip curled. "I was driving Susie back to Bristol. She'd had a lot to drink, and she told me everything. All about my little girl: how cute she was, and how she died, all alone in that swimming pool. I think I went a bit crazy. I couldn't think straight."

Libby strained to hear Ned's words through his tears. "I stopped the car, grabbed the satnav and hit Susie with it. It smashed into the side of her head." He rubbed clenched fists into his eyes. "I thought of my little girl, drowning. Susie deserved to find out what it was like for Annie Rose."

He took a breath, shuddering. "I drove to Exham, and carried her out to the beach. It was already blowing a gale. I put her under the lighthouse; tucked her in between the supports. I couldn't kill her. I left it to fate to decide. She might have woken up in time, before the tide came in." He looked at the ring of horrified faces and pleaded, "I didn't kill her."

"How could you do such a thing, Ned?" Samantha hid her face, paper-white, behind her hands. "How could you?"

Ned tears dried. He glowered at his wife, hate in his eyes. "She deserved it. I'd do it again, for Annie Rose."

CHAPTER THIRTY

Max

Libby curled up on the sofa. Max stretched out in an armchair. Both nursed large glasses of wine. Bear and Fuzzy jostled for position on the floor, in front of the fire. Mandy had gone to Bristol with her mother. "I'll be back the moment she starts nagging," she whispered to Libby. "See you tomorrow, probably."

"The town will pay for Susie's headstone," Max said. "It's going to say, *Loving Mother of Annie Rose.* We won't take the money from her estate. Mickey's welcome to it. It won't do him any good."

"Oh? Why not?"

"Think, Libby. He's probably a bigamist. He was still married to Susie, when he went through some sort of a ceremony with his film star wife. I guess he always hoped Susie might die first so he could get his hands on her money. I've already emailed some law-enforcement contacts in California. He'll end up in gaol, I hope, and with any luck, his new wife will sue for damages and he'll be ruined."

It took a while for Libby to stop laughing. "I'm glad about the headstone. I'm sure Annie Rose was all Susie really cared about, in the end."

Max asked, "How did you know Susie was pregnant when she left Exham? You weren't here, then."

"Ever since the day I dressed up in that Victorian costume, at Mangotsfield Hall, I've had a feeling I was missing something. It was the costume, you see. There were layers of clothes; petticoats and skirts and corsets. I think I said, 'I could put on pounds and no one would notice.' The point was, you could hide anything under there. It rang a bell, because my son had told me about one of my husband's ancestors, a maid, who 'got into trouble.' But I didn't put it all together at first. I didn't think about Susie hiding her bump, to trap Mickey into believing he was Annie Rose's father."

Libby took a large mouthful of wine. "About the document I gave you." Max pulled the single sheet of paper out of his pocket. "What do you want to do with it?"

He unfolded it, reading in silence. "You're right about everything," he said, when he finished. "Bert, Mickey, Samantha, Ned. You're right about me, too. I never quite got over Susie. I met my wife in Bath, but the marriage was a mistake. Joe grew up living with my wife. I don't think he ever forgave me, even though she left me. Divorce is tough on a child." He shrugged. "I made my fortune, bought the big house and salted money away in the stock market. But there was always something missing. I guess I craved excitement."

He raised one eyebrow. "When I retired early from the bank, I looked around for something else to do: something that could give me the buzz banking lacked. I'm afraid I can't tell you what I do, or who I work for." He waved the paper at Libby. "I can't comment on your last sentence."

Libby smiled. Not commenting was as good as admitting her conclusions were correct. The last sentence read, *Secret Service*. "I suppose it's because of your job you were so keen for an excuse go to the States. Or were you heading somewhere else?"

"On my way to Bolivia, actually, but you're right. It was useful to have an excuse." Max's smile was enigmatic. Whatever the job description, he was keeping it to himself.

"Tell me about Alan Jenkins. I know he's one of your old mates, but you wouldn't have been able to get him out of trouble with the police, if you didn't have contacts."

"You're quite a sleuth, Libby. The ringing gang was part of a vehicle fraud, where the proceeds were laundered and sent to Latin America, to finance the drug trade. Joe discovered it, and he was on the point of arresting Alan, who had no idea what he was getting into. Joe wasn't too pleased when I stepped in."

"That gave him another reason to be mad at you."

Max drained his glass. "I'm not easy to know, Libby. You'll find that, if you let me stick around." He stood up. "Do you want me to go, now, and let you get on with your new life? What's it going to be: a patisserie or a chocolatier?" Libby's body ached with tiredness. Her brain had all but stopped working, but at least she knew she didn't want Max to disappear from her life.

She took the document from his hand, tore it into small pieces, and tossed them into the fire. "There's a whole lot of things I don't know, but I'll think about it all tomorrow. For now, let's just finish the wine."

Thank you for reading Murder at the Lighthouse. I hope you had fun meeting the inhabitants of Exham on Sea. If you enjoyed the story, please leave a short review on Amazon to let other readers know.

About the author...

Frances Evesham writes mystery stories: the Exham on Sea contemporary crime series set in a small Somerset seaside town, and the Thatcham Hall Mysteries, 19th Century historical mystery romances set in Victorian England.

She collects grandsons, Victorian ancestors and historical trivia, likes to smell the roses, lavender and rosemary, and cooks with a glass of wine in one hand and a bunch of chillies in the other. She loves the Arctic Circle and the equator and plans to visit the penguins in the south one day.

She's been a speech therapist, a professional communicator and a road sweeper and worked in the criminal courts. Now, she walks in the country and breathes sea air in Somerset.

Find out more online at:

www.francesevesham.com

www.twitter.com/francesevesham

www.facebook.com/frances.evesham.writer

If you enjoyed Murder at the Lighthouse, you may like Murder on the Levels, the second Exham on Sea Mystery.

More cosy crime, murder mysteries, clever animals, cake, and chocolate all feature in the second Exham on Sea mystery, set in a seaside town in Somerset.

Two cyclists die on the Somerset Levels, and the Exham bakery gets the blame. Libby Forest runs into danger as she sets out to solve the mystery, save the bakery and rescue her career, helped by Bear, the enormous Carpathian Sheepdog, Fuzzy, an aloof marmalade cat and the handsome, secretive Max Ramshore.

The stories feature a cast of local characters, including Mandy the teenage Goth, Frank the baker and Detective Sergeant Joe Ramshore, Max's estranged son. The green fields, rolling hills and sandy beaches of the West Country provide the perfect setting for crime, intrigue and mystery.

For lovers of Agatha Christie novels, Midsomer Murders, lovable pets and cake, the series offers a continuing supply of quick crime stories, each one short enough to read in one sitting, as Libby and her friends solve a mix of intriguing mysteries.

The Exham on Sea Mysteries:
Contemporary Cosy Crime Fiction
Murder on the Levels

The Thatcham Hall Mysteries:
Victorian Fiction
An Independent Woman
Danger at Thatcham Hall

Free Kindle Ebook:
True Crime
Murder Most Victorian: available from
www.francesevesham.com/murder-most-
victorian

The characters and events described in the Exham on Sea Mysteries are all entirely fictitious. Some landmarks and places of interest may strike my neighbours and fellow residents of Somerset, and particularly of Burnham on Sea, as familiar. I've taken some liberties with a few locations.

72012519R00106

Made in the
USA
Middletown, DE